Licking The Salt Block

Licking The Salt Block

Copyright @ 2018 by Jan Fink

All rights reserved.

Fifth Estate, Post Office Box 116,

Blountsville, AL 35031

First Edition

Graphic Design by Will Fink

Printed on acid-free paper

Library of Congress Control No. 2018956804

ISBN: 9781936533602

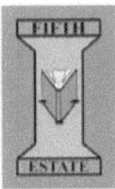

Fifth Estate, 2018

CONTENTS

"All things truly wicked start from an innocence."

~Ernest Hemingway

I was born daughter of Ruby and George Reynolds on the fifth day of December 1949 in Windham Springs, Alabama and given the name Larraine.

My immediate needs were simple. Sustenance, love, bonding, and the inherent will to thrive that does not always come with birth.

I came into the world unaware of earth or sky and of how in the years to come they would follow a collision course.

Licking The Salt Block

Cordie

When Ruby met George Reynolds and fell head over heels for him, I guess I was glad she'd found somebody who could give her all the things her daddy and I couldn't. I'd heard tell of his family. They were landowners with roots based on old money. I think Ruby knew this and saw George as her ticket.

Ruby was my fourth child. She was born undersized with cornflower blue eyes like mine and a taut little February face like her November birth meant nothing to her. She'd come into the world crying more than most babies. It was as if she already wanted the long hard winter to be over. She might not have sensed it at the time, but I was also ready for the end of winter.

There had been hardly enough in the larder the past two months to feed the three children we had afore Ruby came along. The smokehouse stood empty; the meat from the hog we'd slaughtered the fall afore last was gone. Otha hunted ever day, and if luck held, we'd have squirrel, rabbit or deer meat to go along with a pone of cornbread and the last of the turnip and collard greens.

Our last cotton crop had been stolen during the night along with our wagon. We were down to pennies and doing without when Ruby arrived. Come spring I'd borrow seeds from neighbors or charge 'em at the feed store and put twice as many seeds in the ground for the next year. If the crops made, I'd put up twice as many jars of peas, beans, tomatoes and squash.

Looking back I sometimes wonder if I was the cause of Ruby being so high strung. Even as a child she was edgy, always dewy-eyed like she was going to bust out crying if ya gave her the slightest glance. When she spoke at all, it was in a whispery, subdued voice like she didn't really have the need to be heard or the need to share nothing with us. From early age she played only one childhood game. It was a game she made up and unlike any I'd ever knowed a child to play. She'd cover her head with one of my crocheted doilies, wrap a sheet about her shoulders, take my crochet hook and have her sisters kneel before her while she touched their heads with the hook like she was blessing 'em. Her sisters didn't like the game, and pretty soon they'd go running and hiding when they saw Ruby coming dressed up in that sheet with her head covered by the doily. Ruby just kept playing the game by herself. She walked around for hours all dressed up, tapping the furniture with the crochet hook 'til she had blessed ever piece of it in the house. Then she'd go back to the first piece she blessed and start all over.

The morning of Ruby's sixth birthday Otha came in the kitchen with a flour sack, laid it on the kitchen table, opened it and called me to come look inside. At the bottom of that sack all curled up lay the cutest little white and tan bobtail pup I'd ever seen. Otha had this big smile on his face like he'd just made that pup appear outta thin air.

"He's for Ruby. Something she can play with."

"Where'd ya get this little pup?"

"A stray showed up down at Fields Grocery and dropped her litter a few weeks back. Fields already give away the rest of the litter. This little one here was the runt, the last of 'em. Ya think Ruby will like him?"

"Ya did good, Otha. I can't imagine no child that wouldn't want this pup. You can give him to her after we cut her cake this evening."

While the cake cooled, I made some chocolate icing and then went through my sewing kit 'til I found a piece of red ribbon just the right size to tie around the little pup's neck. Otha rekindled the cookstove. When it got good and hot, I put on a pot of deer stew and a pone of cornbread. At dinner that evening Ruby nibbled a little cornbread while pushing her spoon around and around in her stew, eating none of it. She got excited when the time came for cake. She ate her a big piece and then opened the gifts from her sisters. They had drawed pictures for her and wrapped up bobby pins, safety pins and anything else they could find. When all 'em gifts was opened, Otha went out on the back porch and came back in smiling with the flour sack in his hand. He laid it in Ruby's lap.

"I brought ya somebody. This is from me and your mama."

The sack wiggled in Ruby's lap. She started to open it but then hesitated, looking undecided. I thought the pup was gonna wiggle its way off her lap afore Ruby finally opened the sack and looked inside. Didn't no smile cross her lips. She put her thumb and forefinger on her nose and squeezed.

"This thing stinks. You didn't bring me somebody. This ain't nobody."

Otha left the room. I couldn't tell if he was mad or maybe a little heartbroke. Nothing we done for Ruby made her happy.

For the next two years that little dog followed Ruby's ever step, but she paid him no attention. Sometimes she even throwed rocks at him if he got too close. Never even gave him a name other than just yelling, "Get away from me, Nobody!" He was a good little dog, always letting us know if a snake was in the yard. He loved taters. Sometimes I'd boil an extra one and put it in with the table scraps for him at feeding time. He'd just as soon eat 'em raw as cooked, but I felt sorry for him and wanted to treat him once in a while.

One day bout the middle of August I called Nobody to get his supper, but he didn't come running like he always did. I walked round the yard calling him, and when he still didn't show, I left his bowl on the back stoop. It was still there untouched the next morning. For a week and a half there was no sign of him. Otha said he might a got snakebit and died in the woods. I missed the little dog. Ruby never asked about him. Life went on, the days filled with harvesting and putting up for the winter.

The time had come to dig taters. Ruby's sisters were on a stayover with Otha's mama, so we took Ruby to the fields with us early morning to beat the heat. We brought along shovels and a large basket to bring the taters back to the house. While Otha and I dug, Ruby built little stick houses between the rows.

By noon the sun was beating down on us. I stopped long enough to pull up my apron and wipe the sweat off my face, and that's when I saw Nobody at the edge of the field. He was standing there quiet and looking toward us.

"Otha! Look! There's Nobody!"

"Be damned! He smelled these fresh taters."

I picked up one of the taters I'd just dug, wiped the dirt off it, and threw it in Nobody's direction. It fell short, but he didn't go to it, just stood there still as a statue.

I cupped my hands round my mouth and called out, "Nobody! Here, boy! Nobody! Come get this tater!"

He lowered his head and began walking slowly in our direction. Then his pace quickened.

"That a boy! Come on!"

"Cordie! Quit calling him! Get Ruby under the basket now! Hurry! Nobody's gone off and got the rabies!"

For a moment I couldn't believe what I was hearing. I grabbed Ruby, put her under the basket, and then wrapped my arms as far around it as they'd go. Nobody was closer now, and I could see what Otha had sensed. There was a ragged, oozing wound on his right leg, his eyes the size of silver dollars and foam dripping from his mouth covering his chest. His coat was dirty, oily and full of cockleburs. Closer now, he was running straight toward me and the basket. I barely recognized him as that sweet little dog that kept my yard free of snakes.

Otha stepped in between the basket and Nobody, his shovel raised, waiting. I wanted to close my eyes but couldn't. When he got within a few feet Nobody leaped. Otha swung the shovel, knocking him to the side. Nobody got back on his feet and charged toward me and the basket again. Otha swung the shovel, putting Nobody on the ground once more. He got right back up like he didn't feel the hits. Again he charged, his mouth open, making guttural sounds, blood gushing from the strikes about his head. Otha hit him again and this time while he was down, Otha drove the shovel deep into his neck, almost taking his head off. I waited for the next charge, but Nobody was done.

I couldn't move, just sat there trembling and holding tight to the basket while Otha took the shovel and covered Nobody with a mound of dirt and taters from the rows.

"Take Ruby back to the house. Once y'all are out of sight, I'll bury him at the edge of the field."

I lifted the basket, took Ruby's hand and started to the house with her. Ruby broke my grip and ran back to the mound of dirt. She kicked at it, raising dust that swirled, covering her clothes, and then drifted away in the dry summer air. I ran to her and took her hand to pull her away, but she just kept kicking. All the way to the house she kept repeating the same words.

"I told you it ain't nobody! I told you it ain't nobody!"

If I was the cause of Ruby's state, there was nothing I could a done. From birth Ruby wanted more attention and everything else than I could give her. Farm life eats you up with hard work. Hard work and survival was all I'd ever knowed. I never had no different kind of life nor the time to think about one.

So I wasn't surprised when at age eighteen Ruby bought her a one-way-out ticket to a better life with George Reynolds. I've never travelled much, but I do know if ya buy a ticket to anywhere, it don't take ya straight away to where ya going. There are a lot of stops along the way.

I knew a long journey and a hard road lay ahead. George Reynolds' mama Ionia had already done everything she could to halt the relationship 'tween her son and my Ruby. She'd asked questions about Ruby's family background and come to the notion that Ruby and all the rest of us weren't good enough for her boy. So when Ruby got with child, she and George ran off to Mississippi and got married.

When little Larraine was born, Ruby thought she'd be going to live in the big house in town with George and his family. That wasn't to be Ruby's first stop along the way. Ionia refused to let the baby or Ruby in her home. So now they was here on my doorstep, dropped off by George who went on back to his mama Ionia's household.

Ruby

I hated farm life and poverty. My world was hand-me-down clothes, dirt, dust, the smell of animals and wood smoke. We had no electric lighting, no running water, no bathroom. In the summer we baked in the heat. In winter we were never warm. When I reached my teens, I was ready to do anything to get out. Get out and never look back.

Last spring Daddy was offered a wagon, a team of mules and a small sum for my hand in marriage to old Malty, who lived down the road. Malty was fifteen years older than me, and I knew he was looking for a field hand more so than a wife. I didn't do fieldwork for Mama or Daddy, so I sure had no intentions of doing it for old Malty. A wagon, a team of mules, a little money in hand and one less mouth to feed in his household had to be an attractive deal to Daddy. I feared he might take the offer. So I cried and said I'd die before I'd go live with old Malty. The deal was never mentioned again, but there were a lot of good old boys in the country looking for wives and help on their farms. Daddy might take the next offer, so I began saying a nightly prayer that a way out would come soon.

My prayer was answered the next week at school. A group of giggling classmates was all excited about a young man's plans to rent the school auditorium on weekends and show movies. The nearest movie theater was a forty-mile round trip. Not many of the young people in our community had the money or a way to town to see a show. By the end of the day the whole school was buzzing with the news. There was a rumor that the movie man would be at Fields Grocery Saturday to promote his show. It was a three-mile walk from our farm. I planned to be there.

It seemed an eternity before Saturday. I spent the week pulling together my outfit. I'd wear my best skirt and blouse, shine my shoes and try and talk my older sister Ruthie into lending me a pair of her white socks. I didn't sleep at all Friday night. As soon as the sun came up Saturday morning, I was out the door. When I topped the last hill that led down to the grocery, I could see I wasn't the only one that morning who got an early start. The acre lot that surrounded the store was already packed. It looked like the whole countryside had turned out to welcome the young man who was bringing entertainment to our bleak community.

Noon came and went and he hadn't arrived. There wasn't a tree or any shelter on the store lot. The sun beat down, but we all held our places in the crowd, sweating and waiting. People milled about, caught up on gossip and sipped RC colas.

It was three that afternoon when I heard the sound of an engine in the distance. There was little traffic along these country roads. It had to be the movie man. The crowd pressed closer to the road carrying me with it. And there he was. The engine I'd heard was not that of a car. He was riding a big motorcycle.

The crowd parted, giving him a path to the center of the store lot and then everyone closed in around him. He was tall and handsome with hair black as a starless, stormy night, dressed in jeans and a beautiful embroidered western shirt, a red silk bandana around his neck and expensive looking cowboy boots on his feet. And there on his shoulder sat a small monkey with one hand full of flyers and the other resting affectionately on the movie man's head. He got off the motorcycle, and the monkey jumped down from his shoulder and rushed toward the crowd handing out flyers.

I'd never seen a real monkey and hesitated to take the flyer it held up to me. It stood staring with dark round eyes waiting for me to extend my hand. I wanted the flyer, but the monkey frightened me. The movie man told the crowd that the flyer would give us all the information we needed to know about upcoming feature attractions. I stood there frozen, still unable to reach out and take the flyer from the little dark-eyed creature. Movie man approached me, smiling.

"This little guy won't hurt you. His name's Lucky. He's gentle as a lapdog. Lucky, give this pretty little lady a flyer."

Lucky climbed back up to the movie man's shoulder, this time holding the flyer down to me. I smiled and took the piece of paper. In bold print at the top of the page was the name GEORGE REYNOLDS, then the words ROAD SHOWMAN. The rest of the page was filled with movie titles and dates. The monkey scampered away into the crowd handing out more flyers. Movie man was still smiling and looking down at me.

"There now, that wasn't so bad. Hope to see you at my shows."

Then he was off shaking hands and taking photos of the younger kids on his motorcycle with Lucky perched on their shoulders. I began the long walk home clutching the flyer, afraid even a slight breeze might rip it from my hand. I kept looking down at it. Movie tickets were 40 cents, colas and candy bars 5 cents each. I'd be lucky to come up with the price of a ticket. I'd do whatever it took even if I had to help in the fields. I'd save every penny for the tickets and then buy some bobby pins, do my hair like the stars of the movies he'd be showing on the screen. I'd smile and do everything I could to get his attention.

Movie man had a name and title. I knew George Reynolds the Road Showman was my answered prayer, my way out, my ticket.

Ionia

Joe and I had two sons. George was my youngest and, unlike his practical, quiet older brother, George had a wild streak in him. Both of our boys wanted for nothing. Whatever they wished for we found a way to get it. When George wanted a motorcycle, we got it for him. In three weeks' time he lost control on a country gravel road and hit a tree head-on. The Harley was totaled. George suffered serious head injuries, and he needed a metal plate inserted to protect his skull and brain from further damage. It was a long recovery, and there were days when I was sure I'd lose my son. As soon as he was up and about, he wanted another motorcycle. I couldn't refuse him.

Next came a pet monkey, and hard as that wish was to come by, Joe and I found a young spider monkey in Florida and had it shipped in by train. For the first month I wasn't sure if the ugly little thing would survive. By the second month I wasn't sure if I would survive in the same house with it. From the moment we picked it up at the station, it continually shrieked and threw itself against the bars of its cage. If anyone other than George got near the cage, it would reach out, grab a handful of clothing and pull it through the bars, biting and ripping the fabric while letting out that ungodly shrieking noise.

I didn't hold out much hope for the pitiful wild thing, but George was convinced he could tame and train it. He began wrapping it in a towel, taking it out of the cage and walking around the house talking to it 'til it fell asleep in his arms. It did calm down a bit and even stopped throwing itself against the bars of the cage. George named it Lucky, certain that monkey would bring him good fortune.

He purchased a collar and leash and took Lucky on short walks around the house and yard. He taught it to bring Joe the morning paper. It was when he taught Lucky to sit on his shoulder while he took long rides on the Harley that I began to think my son was working on some kind of plan.

Lucky faithfully brought Joe the morning paper but still had spells of shrieking and unpredictable behavior. Joe rarely took notice of anything to do with his home or children, always leaving that job to me. But he was tired of the whole situation and let me know that getting George the monkey had been a big mistake. So it was me George approached with the plan that I already suspected. He wanted to start his own business, have his own money. The plan was to be a road showman, taking movies to all the surrounding small communities within a forty-mile radius. He would rent school auditoriums and lunch rooms, and he and Lucky would ride out on his Harley to promote his shows. To carry out this plan he needed a 16-millimeter reel-to-reel projector, a screen, a collection of movies and news shorts. He would also need new clothes, something flashy that would draw attention. He wanted to sell refreshments, so he'd need a cooler for colas and candy bars. And he'd need the loan of our car to carry the equipment on show dates.

It was a long list, but if it would get Lucky out of the house a little more, stop Joe's griping and maybe keep George out of trouble, it was worth it. So I handed over the money. It was to be my second and bigger mistake when it came to giving my son everything he wanted. What I had given him to keep him out of trouble was the very thing that got him into trouble.

George's business as a road showman was a big success. Within the first four months, at every movie showing it was standing room only. Then on one of his promotion trips to Windham Springs he briefly met a girl who began coming to every show. He talked about her often, wanting to bring her home to meet me and Joe. I knew the Windham Springs area. Our family once owned the one hundred forty acres that included the sulfur springs, a store, a dwelling and four rental houses. In 1945 we sold it all and purchased a city block in town to build a new home.

I put George off as far as him bringing the girl home 'til Joe and I could take a drive out to Windham Springs and find out who she was. The old store was still there and being operated by a man named Fields. He was able to tell me all I needed to know.

"There's only one of the four rental houses left standing, Ionia. The man you sold that property to divided the land up and sold a lot of it. A couple that used to sharecrop for your daddy bought the last of them old houses and forty acres. They got most of it planted in cotton and the rest in vegetables for their table. That girl you're asking about has to be one of Otha and Cordie's daughters."

The house he told us about wasn't far. We drove past it on the way home, and my heart just sunk to my knees. Didn't look like it'd been cared for in years. In such bad repair it really didn't look like anybody lived in it or could. A collection of beat-up old mismatched chairs filled the part of the porch that hadn't fallen in. Not a blade of grass in the yard, just dirt that the breeze stirred into mini-whirlwinds. How could a girl from this catch the eye of my son?

Up 'til that moment I had lived my life with pride and was part of the elite Southern social structure. My son had no business hooking up with a girl or family who held no station in life. I was sure this girl saw money in my son. If he brought her up again, I would forbid him to see her.

George

I was living the life. Glad to be out of the house once in a while and out from under the control that Mother held over me with every penny she gave or spent in my direction. Lucky was a quick learner and a crowd pleaser with the young and old. He seemed to enjoy riding the Harley, his tail wrapped around my neck, hand resting on my head and doing his part in the promos by handing out flyers and posing for photos. Lucky did bring me good fortune. I was now doing two shows a weekend. My road showman business was a hit; my pockets full of money and girls in every community.

Ruby was at every show date played at Windham Springs, but I didn't immediately recognize her as the girl who was so afraid of Lucky during my first promotion trip to Fields Grocery. Her hair was different and she had more color in her cheeks. She was the first to arrive and the last to leave. Quiet, almost shy, she was always smiling when she bought her ticket. At every show a lot of girls were trying for my attention, but something about Ruby's smile and the way she stayed in the background attracted me.

I offered her a ride home after a Saturday afternoon show. She turned me down at first, but I kept standing there talking to her 'til she said yes. Lucky wasn't too happy. He was used to riding solo with me. He kept his head turned, looking back at Ruby instead of the road ahead. When we reached her home, she said it would be best if I dropped her off at the top of the dirt lane that led to her house, so I obliged. I could see the farmhouse and I understood. It was a pretty rough-looking place. I felt sorry for her.

I started taking her home after each show and made the trip to Windham Springs two or three times during the week to see her. She finally invited me to meet her parents; they were good country folks. I wanted Ruby to meet my family and asked Mother if I could bring her for dinner, but she never agreed to it. Things with me and Ruby were getting serious, and so was Lucky. I knew from the first time Ruby rode the Harley with us that he wasn't happy sharing the seat with her. Lucky had never bitten anyone, but now he had started pulling at Ruby's hair, and when that didn't keep her off the bike, he resorted to scratching and biting. Ruby refused to ride with Lucky and said I had to make a choice.

She convinced me to let Lucky go by offering to be my new sidekick, handing out flyers and posing for photos and anything else I needed, as long as Lucky was no longer along for the rides. Selling Lucky was one of the hardest things I'd ever had to do. When I shipped him to his new owner, he clung to my arms as I crated him. In my mind I can still hear him shrieking and see his terrified face as the porter loaded him on the train.

But I loved Ruby. I did this for her.

If Ruby was to be my sidekick, she had to look the part and draw attention. We decided to go with the Western theme I was already using. I dipped into my pocket and ordered a white Western-cut blouse with sequins and fringes along the shoulders, a white flowing skirt, white hat, red Western boots, and a red silk bandana like mine. Ruby was as beautiful as Dale Evans, like she'd stepped right off the screen of one of my movies.

I missed Lucky, but Ruby was as much of a draw with the crowds as he had been. As soon as we arrived at any promo or show, she was surrounded by the boys. Even those who knew Ruby in her own town couldn't get over the transformation. She was asked out on dates and offered rides home, but it was always me who picked her up and took her home.

Mother was surprised when I sold Lucky. I told her he bit someone and I was afraid he'd become a liability. I didn't tell her it was Ruby he bit, but leaving out that detail did me no good. Mother had ears and eyes in Windham Springs. She already knew Ruby had taken Lucky's place.

"I know it was that girl you've been seeing that Lucky bit. That monkey has more sense than you do. You should have gotten rid of the girl and kept the monkey. I was hoping you'd tire of her, but looks like you've lost all sense. I'll tell you this, George Reynolds, you are not seeing that girl anymore. She'll never be welcome in my house."

There it was. That arrogance born of pride that Mother used to push her way and everyone else through life. If she was worried about me going down in social status by being with Ruby, she needed to take inventory of her own life. Her marriage to my father didn't push her up the social ladder. If anything it brought her down a few rungs. Joe had already sold all the property she had inherited. Now he was talking about selling the lots surrounding our home in town. He called it being enterprising, but, fact was Father was just broke and needed the money. Social status is expensive to maintain.

When I was eleven, Mother had an affair, and when her indiscretion was discovered, she attempted suicide. Father took me and my brother to her bedside to plead with her not to die. When she recovered, it was like none of it had ever happened. Mother had a way of making any unpleasant or socially incorrect parts of life disappear. Now she wanted Ruby to disappear. If anything it made me even more determined to be with Ruby.

Ruby and I continued with the shows and met three times a week for long rides on the Harley. The ears and eyes of Windham Springs reported back to Mother, and she chained my Harley to the big oak in our backyard.

The family car was also off limits 'til, in Mother's words, I came to my senses. It didn't stop me. I hitched rides and saw Ruby as often as I could. The same day Mother told me that she had sold the Harley, Ruby told me she was pregnant. I had lost my Harley, my business and income, and had a baby on the way. Ruby dropped out of school and stayed home feeling sick and looking poorly. In her eighth month we did what we thought would make her parents and mine happy. I was able to borrow a car and we went to Mississippi to get married.

We'd done what we thought was right, but when Larraine was born a month later, the marriage certificate and a granddaughter did not soften Mother's heart. She refused to let Ruby and the baby into her home. I could continue to live there, and she would support me, but not my wife and child. I had no choice but to take the baby and Ruby back to the farm and her mama, Cordie.

Otha

Cordie was a widder with two little girls when I met her. That summer I was hired on to work a corn crop down by the river. By noon the day was scorching hot, and I'd gone down to the river's edge to throw some water on my face and cool down. There she was across the water washing out clothes in the shallows. I called out to her but she ignored me and went on washing and wringing. When she was done she picked up her basket and went down the path into the woodland like I was invisible. I made a point to be at that spot once a week and kept on trying to strike up a conversation with her, but it took three weeks for her to look up, wave and smile.

It took another three weeks yelling across the water afore she told me where she lived and agreed to go with me to a barn dance. When I first seen her up close I knowed I was lovestruck. Her eyes was such a velvety, true light blue ya could damn near see right through 'em. She was soft spoken, didn't talk as much as most women and was a pleasure to be around. We kept company 'til the end of the year and then married. She didn't want to live near the river no more, said it was the river that took her first husband. I found us a place further out in the country. The house weren't much, but we could sharecrop the forty acres of land it sat on and someday maybe buy it.

A year after we settled on the farm Ruthie was born and a year later Ruby. Four girl young'uns in my household and not a one of 'em to be a good hand at helping with the farmwork. Cordie worked alongside me as hard as any man, and she took good care of the young'uns, but not once had she said "I love ya" to me or any of 'em girls. One evening Cordie and me was coming in from the fields and I had to know. We'd been chopping cotton all day, was hot and dirty walking along with the hoes slung up on our shoulders, and I turned to her with my question.

"Cordie. Ya love me and 'em girls?" She nodded her head up and down.

"Then why don't ya ever say it? Why don't ya say I love ya?"

"Cause 'em was the last words I said to my first husband when he climbed in that boat down at the river hoping to catch us a mess of fish for supper. Noon a that day came one of the worst rainstorms I ever seen. Water was standing everywhere and I knowed the river was rushing. He didn't come home that evening or any evening for the next three weeks. The river had took him down and held him 'til it spit him up along the bank miles from where he set out. The men who found him brought him home in their wagon. Least they said it was my husband but what they brought me didn't even look human. That's why I won't ever again say 'em words to anyone I care about."

I never brought it up again. We went on about working the farm and raising 'em girls. The older three weren't much trouble and tried to help me and Cordie with the chores, but from the beginning Ruby was different. I'd never say it out loud to Cordie, but they was something off about Ruby. The older she got the worse she got. Weren't no way to make her happy.

So when Ruby hooked up with George Reynolds I thought she'd made a good match. It was pretty clear the boy came from a family of money. But when they married that one less mouth to feed that I expected turned into four years of one more mouth to feed. Ionia had him drop off Ruby and the baby at our doorstep like they was nothing more than a cast-off dog or cat somebody didn't want. Cordie would never turn away one of her own so 'em staying with us was set in stone. Didn't matter how I felt about it; she took Ruby and the baby in. That same night I put George out, back on the same road where he had picked up Ruby and sent him back to Ionia telling him to never show his face again.

Ruby didn't take to mothering. She sat by the fireside, wrung her hands and cried ever time the baby cried. The slightest noise outside sent her straight up out of her chair running to the door and looking out the windows, sure that it'd all been a dream and George had come back for her. She stayed so worked up her milk wouldn't let down. The baby was crying day and night. Cordie said it was cause the poor child wasn't able to nurse and it was just starving. We'd had young nervous heifers in the past not able to nurse their first calves, and Cordie had to bottle feed 'em to keep 'em living. So she scalded out the same bottle she'd nursed 'em calves with, warmed some milk from the morning milking, and sat by the fire with Larraine resting on her belly bottle-feeding.

In a week's time Larraine gained some weight and didn't cry no more than a normal healthy baby. The same wasn't true with Ruby. She just got worse ever day. She left Cordie in total care of her child. Most days she didn't seem to know the baby as her own. Cordie and I feared Ruby had lost her mind.

Two months passed and one evening coming back from the barn lot there was a new car parked in front of the house. When I got close I could see it was George standing on the porch with Cordie. It made me so damn mad. I was ready to put him back on the road, but Cordie pulled me aside, telling me it was his wife and child and that he had a right. As far as I was concerned George had lost his right two months ago when he dumped 'em. Cordie said he'd brought some money to help care for Ruby and the baby and that he would bring as much as he could ever week if we'd let him see 'em. I wasn't any less mad, but Cordie was right. No matter how mad I was I couldn't begrudge him seeing his wife and child, and Lord knows a little extra money would help. So we let him in and for the next four years he visited once a week and, as he promised, brought a little money.

On one of his visits he brought news that Ionia wanted to see the baby. We all felt hopeful that her wanting to see Larraine might mean she was opening her arms and home to her son's family. They left for town, Ruby in the front seat next to George nervously holding the child she had hardly laid claim to since its birth. Cordie and I went about the day's work and waited for what we hoped would be good news when they returned.

I should have learned my lesson on hope a long time ago. I been hopeful that the seeds I put in the ground would bring a crop, only to watch 'em lay in the ground and never sprout. Being hopeful and wishful thinking don't get ya nowhere in life. They got home late afternoon and George came in holding Larraine. He handed her to Cordie, and then asked me to help him get Ruby out of the car. It hadn't gone well at all. Ionia had refused to let Ruby in her house or even sit out front in the car. She had George drop her off on a street corner downtown while she visited with him and the baby. Ruby was holding the inside door handle, refusing to leave the car, crying and screaming that she was going with George. It took me and George both to get her out of the car and in the house.

Ruby really went down after that. She took a little notebook and wrote in all the days of the months for every coming year 'til she ran out of pages. She spent her days staring down at it, checking off the days 'til George's next visit. With every weekly visit Ruby was convinced she was going home with George. George stopped taking her for rides so we wouldn't have to drag her screaming and crying out of the car. We all tried talking to Ruby, telling her there wasn't no place for her to go home to with George. It didn't do no good; Ruby's mind just kept going down.

As Ruby went down, Larraine thrived. When she started walking she'd hold to Cordie's coattail and go ever where she went. Cordie picked peas and wild blackberries and churned butter with Larraine on her hip or trailing behind her ever step. When it was time to pick cotton Cordie laid her on the cotton sack and drug her up and down the rows as she picked and Larraine slept. It was the same with me. In the evening when I come in from the fields she'd hold her little arms up wanting on my knee for a game of ride a little horsey. And there we'd go, me bouncing her up and down singing out the rhyme.

Ride a little horsey,
Ride 'em downtown.
Ride a little horsey,
Horsey fall down.

We taught her not to touch the woodburning stove. In the fall with the first lighting of the fireplace I thought that child was gonna walk right into the flames. She was curious about everything and afraid of nothing. That's the way life was up 'til her fourth birthday.

Ruby was pregnant again. This time George stepped up. Found 'em a little house for rent in town and started making plans for the move. Didn't take long for Ruby to pack. She took that little notebook where she'd spent the last four years marking off days and threw it in the fire, watching it burn while Cordie begged her to leave Larraine with us 'til she and George got settled. There was no reasoning with Ruby. She was leaving with George, another baby in her belly and taking Larraine. She'd finally got everything she wanted. Maybe that made her feel motherly but I had my doubts that anything would change. Cordie had been that child's mama and I had been her daddy.

The day they left, Larraine held to Cordie's dress afraid to get in the car. Ruby pried her fingers loose and put her in the front seat 'tween her and George. We watched her leaving and could hear her crying all the way down the lane. The car turned onto the main road, leaving us standing there empty.

Larraine

I was terrified when Ruby pulled me from Cordie's arms and took me away from her, Otha, the farm, and the only life I knew. George and Ruby took me back for visits, but when time came to leave, I wanted to stay, crying and holding to Cordie's apron. It made Ruby mad and she stopped the visits, telling me I could see Cordie and Otha when I learned that she and George were my mama and daddy and not them. So I called Ruby and George Mama and Daddy and held my tears when they allowed me visits to the farm. But I still missed Cordie and Otha and wanted more than anything to be back there with them.

When we got settled in the rental house Ionia picked me up once a month for a brief visit. She refused to come to our door. She'd have Daddy and me wait for her out front on the curb. During the visits she asked me lots of questions about Mama. She wanted to know what Mama looked like, if she kept a clean house and cooked good meals. I always said yes. When I got home Mama wanted to know about the visit and when I told her of Ionia's questions it made Mama really mad.

On some visits Ionia would take me to town and buy me a new outfit. She'd toss my old clothes in the garbage and have me change into the new clothes before she took me home. This made Mama even madder. When I returned home Mama would have me change clothes and she'd toss the new outfit in the garbage. It was really confusing.

I didn't like the new house in town. It had no fireplace and only one tall tree in a tiny yard. I did have a new friend there that no one else could see. His name was Duda. We had long talks and played hide-and-seek, jumped rope and built a little fort at the edge of the yard. I had to watch Duda all the time to keep him from running out in the street, climbing too high in the tall tree, or getting hurt in other ways. Mama thought there was something wrong with my mind and wanted to take me to a doctor. Cordie told Mama to let me be. She said Duda was an angel visiting me. An angel that was sent to teach me how to take care of the little brother that would soon come. When Little Brother came home from the hospital, Duda stopped coming to play. I still went to our fort and waited for him every day, but he never came back.

Little Brother was born with troubled legs. By the time he was walking, the doctors put metal braces on them. He clanked about the house bumping into furniture and fell each time he tried to run. I watched over Little Brother as I had watched over Duda, trying to keep him from harm.

The first two years we spent in the rental house, my visits with Ionia became more frequent. By the end of the second year I was already tall for my age and my features were those of George and Ionia. It must have become apparent to Ionia that Mama, my new baby brother and I weren't going away, and just maybe her genes had passed along enough pride in me to demand that we would no longer be ignored. On my visits I asked that we all come, and when Ionia refused I began staying home. After a month of this she agreed to a short, somewhat cold visit with us all.

We sat in her parlor on stiff gold velvet upholstered chairs. Ionia had covered the seats with towels like we might leave a trace of our visit. She didn't make eye contact with Mama or Little Brother, just sat there across from us, hands in her lap and her shoulders as stiff as the parlor chairs. She called Grandfather Joe from the kitchen and introduced him to his daughter-in-law and grandson. He looked uncomfortable and nodded in their direction, then turned to Ionia.

"What's that on the boy's legs?"

"I was about to ask the same thing."

They both looked to Mama. She shuffled in her chair, straightened the wrinkles in her skirt and finally found her voice.

"They're braces. He was born with crippled legs."

"Do you know what causes that?"

Mama ran her hands across the skirt wrinkles again and picked at imaginary lint along the hem. Ionia cleared her throat, showing impatience. Joe lost interest and left the room, going back to the kitchen without saying good-bye, nice to meet you, or excuse me. Mama watched him leave the room, then in a weak voice answered.

"No, Ma'am. I only know he was born that way."

"There's never been a cripple in George's family line. I suspect he's a cripple due to poor nutrition. Poor nutrition that was passed on by your parents to you and by you to my son's children. I'll have some recipes and menus ready for you when you visit again."

With that said we were dismissed, on our way, Mama crying and Little Brother clanking his way down the sidewalk wanting to know who the white-haired lady was. The visits continued with the chairs always covered in towels and a cool air of toleration. Then like turning a page Ionia came around to acceptance. Acceptance that was just as powerful as her rejection had been. Within months she was making plans to build a home for us. It would be adjacent to her house on three large lots she'd stopped Grandfather Joe from selling. Even in this gesture of acceptance she drew the line on Mama's input having anything to do with her new home. It was Ionia who designed and decorated the house with dark floral wallpaper, hardwood floors, and rich heart pine paneling in the kitchen.

Even the landscape was Ionia's design. Our yard became an extension of her yard. No grass, only paths that ran in and around bed after bed of hollyhocks, milkweed, elephant ears, mimosas, and hibiscus. She marked off a plot for vegetables and throughout the rest of the property set out pear, apple, peach, and plum trees.

She also redesigned us. She bought shirtwaist dresses for Mama, little suits and ties for Little Brother, and frilly starched dresses with scratchy petticoats and patent leather shoes for me. I hated the shoes, petticoats and frilly dresses. I wanted to be back on the farm, walking the woods barefoot, wearing the flour sack dresses Cordie made for me.

With the finish of "our" home and landscaping, Ionia held a housewarming to introduce us to her neighborhood. She instructed Mama on what to serve, what to wear, where to stand, and what to say to each person as they arrived. The change was hard for us, like we'd been plopped down on some foreign land and now had to act and speak differently. The change was as easy for Ionia as tearing pages from a sad chapter in a history book and then writing her own story where she played the part of doting mother, mother-in-law and grandmother.

Since leaving the farm, and while in the rental house, Mama had slowly become more attentive and happy, but two years in our new house took that out of her. The house may have been a gift, but it was still Ionia's house. Even the smallest detail of daily life was her decision. She made up weekly menus of Daddy's favorite foods and even went so far as to do the shopping. She told Mama that his favorite dessert was banana pudding but only she could make it the way her son liked it. She arrived each evening with a dish of it. Daddy tired of the pudding and starting throwing it in the garbage. There was no limit to Ionia's control. She went through our garbage can and by morning she was at the back door with banana pudding dripping from her clenched fist demanding to know why her son's dessert had been thrown away.

Mama was again as unhappy and distant as she had been on the farm. There were constant arguments with Daddy caught in the middle, Ionia demanding that Mama do this or do that, and Mama demanding that Ionia leave us alone. When the fights started, Little Brother and I would retreat to the yard. We'd break limbs from the mimosa and build little huts and make costumes out of the hibiscus and elephant ears. We pretended to be stranded on an island, and the voices coming from our house were wild animals deep in the jungle. As long as we stayed in our hut, we were safe.

Daddy got on at the fire department. He worked four days on and three days off. He tried to quiet the rift between Ionia and Mama by taking Mama to the Grand Ole Opry and on a shopping trip while in Nashville. They brought home a chalkware horse for me and a chalkware cowboy for Little Brother. We took pictures, posing with our gifts in the front yard.

He took us to the Birmingham Zoo. Mama packed a picnic of boiled eggs with bacon, lettuce and tomato sandwiches wrapped in waxed paper, pralines, and a big thermos of sweet tea. We ate under the shade of one of the big trees, then walked the trails looking down into pits filled with lions, bears, seals and alligators. Daddy's favorite exhibit was Monkey Island. He told me and Little Brother it reminded him of an old friend. That year Daddy even managed to get tickets to "Cliff's Clubhouse" at a television station where Little Brother and I got to be part of a live audience. The thirty-minute show was

Popeye cartoons and Cousin Cliff amazing us with his magic tricks.

They were good times, but once we were home Mama retreated back to unhappiness. Ionia was ready to redesign me and Little Brother again. She'd decided that we were to be gospel entertainers. She told Mama we needed to be learning music and how to sing at a young age. The younger we started, the better we'd be when we grew up. She would buy the instruments and pay for lessons, and when we began performing she'd have outfits specially made for us. Mama refused the offer. No matter how hard Ionia pushed the plan, Mama stood steady. The refusal made things worse between the two of them. They rarely spoke or looked in one another's direction.

Daddy's job as a fireman was going good. He made a lot of friends. They all enjoyed playing dominos so Daddy decided to have games once a week at our house. He bought a card table, a set of ivory dominos, beer, cigars and snacks, and invited his buddies over. Little Brother and I were allowed to watch 'til bedtime. I loved watching the excitement. They made penny bets, and when the game got close they'd slam the dominos down on the table, making a loud whacking sound.

Mama didn't like Daddy having friends or the weekly domino games. She was miserable under Ionia's control, and I guess she resented him having fun, wanting him to be just as miserable as she was. She went to Ionia and told her Daddy was bringing beer in the house, having loud men over, playing games, placing bets and losing his hard-earned money. For the first time in their relationship Mama and Ionia found common ground.

George

We got the fire call at the station about one in the morning. It was a dilapidated old house down by the tracks belonging to a colored family that had a half dozen or more kids. I'd driven by it many times and seen the kids playing out front. The house was made of pine and already in full blaze when we got there. On the road out front a woman held three little kids with one arm and frantically waved with the other. The hair on the right side of her head was burned off. The burns continued down her neck and right arm. She grabbed at our uniforms, begging for help.

"I got four more babies in there! They in back of the house! My husband is in there a-trying to get them! Please! Save my babies!"

One of my buddies took her and the children across the road and tried to comfort her, giving what first aid he could while waiting for the ambulance. The chief and two other firemen entered the house through the front hall as the rest of us worked the hoses on the left wall of the house. A sudden gust of wind picked up red hot embers, swirling and carrying them to new locations, pushing the flames higher. The heat was unbearable, blistering our faces. As the left side of the house began to cave in, they brought out the husband. His clothing was burned away from the waist up. He was still breathing but didn't look human. I'd never smelled burning flesh. It was a smell so strong I could taste it. Sickly sweet and unpleasant, a combination of charcoal and burning rubber.

They carried the man across the road toward his wife and children. His eyelids were burned away, leaving nothing but a staring, wide-eyed milky look on a lump of burned flesh that had once been his face. As they reached the other side of the road the chief was yelling over his shoulder, "George! Where's the goddamn ambulance!? Get the hoses to the back of the house! Look for the rest of the kids!"

We focused the hoses on the rear walls of the house. The flames had already taken the back porch. The outer right wall moaned, trembled and shifted downward. It landed in a heap, kicking up a cloud of black smoke, more red embers and ashes. Underneath it I saw a small leg protruding from the space between the wall and ground. I dropped my hose; grabbed the tiny leg and pulled. The flesh came away in my hand exposing bone.

An old space heater was later thought to have caused the fire. The husband did not survive. Four children perished in the flames. Five members of one family lost, just trying to stay warm.

After all of that, I came home after my shift to find Mother and Ruby in the living room. They were never comfortable in the same room together, so my first thought was something had happened to one of the kids.

I was wrong. Ruby sat quietly by as Mother laid down the law. No more domino games and betting, no more beer in the house, and if I wanted to spend time with my friends I would have to do it elsewhere. She went on to say how bad it would look if neighbors saw me bringing alcohol in a house where kids lived and that all the cars parked out front of the house and men laughing and yelling would give them the impression a wild party was going on.

Ruby may have sat there quiet, not once uttering a word, but I knew she had put Mother up to this. She'd complained about the games from day one. Said the noise was keeping her and the kids up at night and giving her a headache. Hell, the kids loved watching us play and wanted to learn the game, and as far as giving Ruby a headache, that was impossible. She always had a headache.

It was nothing more than an innocent once-a-week domino game with fellow workers, but I was just too tired to defend myself. I was worn out and numb, tired of this shit between Mother and Ruby. For years I had been their referee. Now they were tag-teaming me, set on my destruction. They had the advantage. I had no partner. Femme fatales working, whittling me away. They'd taken my road showman business and Lucky, who was always faithful and more loving than Mother or Ruby had ever been. Now I was being told I could not even invite friends into my own home.

You can see why I didn't bother to argue with Mother or Ruby. It didn't seem to make any difference. I just sat there with the smell of burning flesh still in my hair and in the back of my throat. I couldn't see Mother or Ruby, just that child's leg falling apart in my hand. If our neighbors had been at the fire and seen me and my buddies fighting to save home and life, I wondered if they would still have a problem with a game of dominos and a few beers. To hell with them.

Larraine

Mama got what she wanted. Daddy joined her state of misery. Along with his four days working at the fire department he started a part-time business repairing televisions and radios and installing television antennas. He arranged a work space in the garage with big tables, bins and Mason jars, their lids nailed up to the rafters. The jars held little tubes, knobs and screws. When he wasn't fighting fires he was in the garage hunched over one of the big tables sorting through a mound of contents from the bins and jars. There were no more family outings or communication, just dead cold silence in the house. There were days when, after he finished working in the garage, he'd leave and come home late at night or sometimes not come home at all.

Out of necessity Daddy was pulled back into family communications. The doctors felt that Little Brother's legs were straight and removed the braces. In a week's time he slipped on a throw rug and broke his left leg. He couldn't manage crutches so a wheelchair was brought in. When the cast was taken off, he stumbled over a root in the backyard and broke his right leg. The wheelchair was brought back in, and this time the doctors decided that as soon as the leg healed, surgery would have to be done on both legs to put in pins to strengthen them.

Before the operation there were weekly trips to the Crippled Children's Clinic in Birmingham. After the surgery the living room was cleared of furniture and replaced with a hospital bed. He was confined to the wheelchair and bed for another year.

I spent time up on the bed with him playing paper dolls and making art by cutting out pictures from magazines and pasting them down on construction paper. Little Brother always cut out pictures of trees and grass. All his art pictures were of things outdoors. I guess that's where he wanted to be.

There were days when I played out front and would look up to see him in his wheelchair at the big picture window catching flies with his hands. He'd tap on the window, hold up his clenched fist, smile and open his fist, releasing the fly he'd just caught. It would buzz away and then return to the window to be his captive once more. I felt so sorry for him. His life the past two years mirrored that of the fly. Free, running and playing, and then back captive to his wheelchair and bed. The doctors told Mama and Daddy that Little Brother would never be able to play any contact sports, but the pins would make his legs stronger and he'd be walking normal.

When Little Brother healed, the wheelchair and hospital bed were taken away and the living room furniture put back in place. We had a little party in his honor with cupcakes and lemonade. To show everyone that he was back to health Little Brother entertained us with his imitation of Elvis Presley singing "Hound Dog." He swiveled his legs and hips while belting out, "*You aint-a-nuthin but a hound dog.*" Every time he sang out the word "You", he'd point at us. We laughed so hard he repeated his performance four times.

I can't recall laughter in the house after that afternoon. Little Brother was back, but so was the silence. Daddy retreated to the garage, spending all his time there when not at the fire station. The late nights coming home got later, the silence again broken by arguments between him and Mama. Little Brother and I began spending most of our time out of the house. During the week we went next door to Ionia's, and on weekends and summers we were sent to the farm to stay with Cordie and Otha.

Ionia seemed to enjoy the time we spent with her. There were always fresh, warm cookies and milk waiting for us. Some afternoons she'd whisper in Little Brother's ear, telling him stories that made him giggle. She had mellowed, but this change in her behavior was sudden and odd and out of character for Ionia. She was changing in other ways, too. It was like she no longer held to the past and her upbringing. She was reinventing herself. She freed herself of social confines and scoffed the norm. She was well respected in our neighborhood, but neighbors whispered that she was different now, maybe even a little crazy.

Ionia would wait 'til the first spring rain to plant her garden. Little Brother and I would watch from our bedroom window as she walked along the rows poking her finger into the rich earth and dropping the seed. Her mixed-breed dog, Mac, would follow behind. When the last seed was in the ground with rain still falling, she'd sit soaking wet at the edge of the garden plot, Mac resting his head in her lap.

She stopped believing in conventional medicine and refused to go to the doctor for any reason. She began using old home remedies, even some that she herself concocted but that rarely worked. One afternoon while she was hacking a stubborn root of the mimosa, the butcher knife she was using missed its mark and cut her finger to the bone. She slowed the bleeding with a tourniquet, rubbed the area with her homemade salve and stitched up the wound with needle and thread from her sewing basket.

Her days going to the hairdresser stopped; she let her hair grow long and wild around her face. She became unconcerned with fashion and cleaned her closets of expensive dresses, giving them to the needy and some to me to play dress-up. Afterwards I never saw her in anything other than plain house dresses with bibbed aprons. The pockets of the aprons were always filled with seeds and the peppermints she gave me and Little Brother when we helped in the garden. More often than not her house dress was inside out, the label flapping in the wind along with her long, white hair.

She bought eight peacocks and let them roam freely about the yard. They hid in the beds of elephant ears and hibiscus, rushing out screaming with their tail feathers raised, chasing me, Little Brother and any stray dog or cat that had the misfortune to wander onto our property. A caged mynah bird was delivered and kept in the house. It learned to speak in Ionia's voice and knew us all by name.

That summer I told Cordie about the change in Ionia.

"What's your mama, George and Grandfather Joe think about it?"

"They don't say much to one another, but I heard Mama on the phone one day talking to the next-door neighbor. Mama said, 'I know. Everybody on the block is talking about her. I think she's gone nuts, full-blown crazy.'

"If Grandfather Joe has noticed the change, he hasn't mentioned it to anybody. He has little to say about anything, just sits in his den all day smoking his pipe."

"Your grandmamma Ionia may be different, but I don't think she's lost her mind. Sometimes when a body goes to acting that way it's cause of something they done or didn't do in the past. To make up for whatever it was that has laid on their chest for a long time, they go in a different direction. They do the reverse of what they done afore. Everything about their life takes on an opposite nature and meaning. Ionia just become a contrary, and sometimes that's a good thing."

It was a good thing. I was glad Ionia had become a contrary. It allowed her to see how bad things were in our home and with Mama and Daddy. On warm summer afternoons when her gardening was finished, she would tell us stories and read our fortunes with a deck of playing cards. She knew when we were sad or troubled. In a soft voice she'd say, "Close your eyes and I will teach you to fly. You are as light as the mynah bird; spread your wings and take to the sky. Do you see the trees below you? Are you gliding on the wind? If you grow weary, you can rest on the clouds."

The words of the contrary took us away. And fly we did.

Cordie

Ruby's ticket got her off the farm but not to the destination she was hoping for. Ruby got George, a new home with electrical lighting, an indoor toilet and even a new car of her own, but none of it brought her no happiness. I knew what was going on 'tween her and George. One of our neighbor women had a husband that beat on her. No matter how much makeup Ruby put on her face or her wearing 'em Hollywood dark sunglasses, she didn't fool me none. George was beating on her. She was sending the kids to us every weekend when school was in and they spent summers with us. Otha and I was glad to have 'em. Larraine was ten years old now and had grown like a wild shrub, tall and looking more like George ever day. Her little brother already looked a lot like George, too. Each time we called him by name, Larraine would correct us, saying, "No don't call him that. He's Little Brother." So we all called him Little Brother.

Little Brother was full of mischief. The first summer he spent with us one of my hens had fifteen hatchlings. I'd kept 'em up in a pen and fed and watered 'em ever day. I went out one morning, and ever one of 'em poor little chicks was hanging by

Licking The Salt Block

their necks in the holes of the chicken wire. I questioned Little Brother and he said it looked like they'd run into the fence and hung themselves. I knew that not to be the truth; some of 'em was hanging as high as three feet up. He finally 'fessed up and told me he had throwed rocks at 'em, and realizing what he'd done, he hung 'em up in the wire hoping I wouldn't know no difference. I didn't whip him, but we had us a good long talk, and he cried, promising never to do it again. I put such a scare on him he was afraid of chickens after that. He wouldn't even use the outhouse 'til Larraine chased away the chickens that stayed under it, scratching for bugs and looking up through the diamond-shape hole ya sat on to do your business.

The kids didn't talk about Ruby and George or what was going on at home, but the signs were there. Larraine was quiet like there was something always on her mind. Otha feared her heart had turned yellah like the flowers of the bitterweed that grew wild in our pastures, made our cow's milk sour and killed 'em if they ate enough of it. When a sudden summer storm rolled in, the first clap of thunder sent Little Brother running and hiding in the closet. It was sad to see young'uns in that state of mind.

We did our best to get 'em happy. At night Otha would build a fire. We drug stumps from the woodpile, used 'em as chairs

57

and roasted weenies on sticks and ate 'em folded up in a piece of white bread. When we were all full, Otha told tall tales about his adventures with witches, gypsies and lightning bugs. It was the medicine 'em kids needed. Otha had 'em laughing and making up their own stories.

Our well went dry that summer. I took Larraine to the woodland with me to find a piece of willow wood. Otha got a shovel and we all took to the woodland with me in front, witchin' for water as my mama had done when I was a child. It was slow going. We must a walked nearly the whole forty acres afore the willow wood started to point down and quiver in my hand. Otha started digging on that spot and four feet down water started trickling into the hole. Larraine and Little Brother thought I'd just done magic. I gave Larraine the witchin' rod and told her ever woman for generations in my family had the gift to find water and maybe the gift would be passed along to her. She walked all the way back to the house holding the willow wood, sure she'd find us more water.

Otha taught Larraine the ways of his Cherokee mama. They took long walks in the woodland, him showing her how to walk without making a sound, how to track and how to build teepee shelters from the limbs of pines. He shared his mama's wisdoms about the bond 'tween human beings and four-leggers and how we should respect 'em. Sometimes Larraine would come back from their walks in the woodland cradling a baby rabbit in her hands, its breath ragged, heart pounding, near death. She nursed three that summer. One died the first day, but the other two thrived and she took 'em back to the spot in the woodland where she found 'em and let 'em go.

Otha taught her the "Cherokee Morning Song." Larraine was up at dawn ever morning with Otha. As they walked to the barn to feed the livestock, they would sing out their greeting to the spirit world.

We n' de ya ho, We n' de ya ho,
We n' de ya, we n' de ya ho ho ho ho,
He ya ho, he ya ho, ya ya ya.

Larraine loved her time with us. She remembered ever lesson we taught her and was always hungry for more. Our neighbor's kids had horses and they'd ride over sometimes to visit. Larraine would run down the lane to meet 'em, and one of the boys would swing her up behind him and bring her on to the house. Sometimes they'd hand her the reins and let her ride about the yard. Then they'd have races starting at the top of the lane and ending back at the house. We'd all sit on the porch watching to see which horse would be the fastest. I watched the look on Larraine's face, too, and knew it wasn't one of the boys but the horses that were to be her first love.

Summer was at end. Me and Otha dreaded the kids going back home to what we knew was a bad situation and getting worse ever day. Ruby came to pick 'em up the Sunday afore they was to start back to school. We had to call Larraine up from the woodland. She'd left early that morning; I knew she was out there walking the forty acres that were as familiar to her now as taking a breath. When Larraine climbed into the car with Ruby, the look on her face made me think that Otha's fears were coming true. That the bad situation at home 'tween Ruby and George was turning Larraine's heart yellah and poisonous, like the flowers of the bitterweed.

Larraine

Before we got out of the car Mama told us Daddy wasn't feeling good and we should get our baths and go to our bedroom 'til supper. There was music coming from inside the house. All the way to the front door Little Brother kept asking Mama, "What's that? What's that?"

"Something your daddy bought. Get inside and do what I told you."

I thought we'd stepped into the wrong house. The living room had been cleared of furniture, lamps, and even the pictures on the wall of me, Little Brother, Mama and Daddy posing in the front yard with our souvenirs from the Grand Ole Opry. It was all replaced by a big oak console stereo and one eggshell white leather chair. Daddy was sitting in it with an ashtray in his lap looking straight ahead, blowing smoke from his cigarette.

Little Brother ran to the stereo, rubbing his hand along the smooth oak finish. Daddy told him to get away from it and never touch it again. Mama hurried us out of the room and down the hall to get baths. While in the tub I listened to the words of the song Daddy was playing.

You make my eyes run over all the time
You're happy when I'm out of my mind
You don't love me, but won't let me be
Don't you ever get tired of hurting me?

Each time the song ended Daddy would play it again, raising the volume. I was sure he was talking to Mama through the words of the song. It played through supper, Daddy never coming to the table. As we ate, he made trips back and forth from the living room to the garage. With every trip when he came back inside he replayed the song, raising the volume 'til the kitchen walls throbbed along with the beat of drums and bass guitars. The song played over and over 'til late that night.

I was glad to get back to school the next day and could hardly wait for library time. I checked out as many books as allowed, all about horses. I wanted to know everything about them. I wanted one of my own to ride while at the farm. I decided I'd go to Ionia's after school instead of home. That way I could study the books and when the time was right ask Otha if someday I might have a horse.

Ionia had a housekeeper now who did the cleaning and prepared all the meals so she could devote all her time to her garden and flowers. Ionia called her Toxie because she was cockeyed, her eyes giving the impression that she was always intoxicated. Toxie's life had been a hard one. Her husband had long ago put his mark on her. One night while in an angry rage he'd sliced her left cheek from eye to chin. She was as black as Cordie's cookstove with that ragged shiny scar trailing down her cheek. Her face was like a bad watercolor painting where the colors had run from too much water on the brush, but it didn't seem to bother her. A few years back her husband had died by the same knife that he'd used to slice Toxie's cheek. While in a fight at one of the honkytonks down by the river, the other man took the knife away from him and opened up his throat. Toxie was grateful for her job, a hard worker, soft spoken, gentle, and always smiling like she'd just heard a funny story.

Ionia was in the side yard, hunched over, pulling weeds from the hollyhock beds. Toxie was in the kitchen making a pot of chicken and dumplings.

I came in the kitchen. "Mind if I stay with you for a while?"

"Law no, chile. You want something cool to drink? Think ah got some leftover tea cakes from day afore."

"No, thanks. I just want to read my library books."

"Your mama and daddy in 'nother falling out?"

"Probably. That's all they seem to do these days."

"Miss Ionia sure had hope they mend fences. You stay here long as you like. Miss Ionia won't mind and ah sho don't. Ah likes folks in the kitchen when ah's cooking, make for a sweeter dish." Toxie hummed and added a big chunk of butter to the dumplings.

"You like horses, Toxie?"

"Oh yeah, chile. They's beautiful animals. One of the good Lord's best work."

"You ever have a horse?"

"Nooo. Mah daddy had a ol' mule that pulled the plow and wagon, but we never had no horse."

"I got all these books today about horses. This one's a story called 'The Black Stallion.' You want to see his picture?"

Toxie joined me at the kitchen table, standing over my shoulder, wiping her hands on her apron, looking down at the picture of the black stallion.

"Law! That horse black as me but a whole lot more purty! What his story all about?"

"I can loan you the book when I'm finished."

"Chile, old Toxie can't read."

"Why not?"

"Never went to school. Mah mama and daddy didn't think ah could learn cause of mah aahs. Ah stayed home working the fields 'til ah meet my husband. He mare me and take me off to work his fields. That just the way it was. Lot of us colored chirrens not go to school."

"Well, I'll have supper here in the kitchen with you and read aloud the story about the black stallion."

"No. No. That not let. You eat at the big table in the dining room."

"Why can't I eat where I want to? I want to eat here with you, Toxie, and read to you."

"Colored and white peoples ain't let to eat at the same tables. Don't guess you study in school yet about the big war long time ago 'tween peoples up north and down south. Us colored peoples not thought of as citizens. We was slaves. White peoples in the South didn't think colored peoples had souls and that colored peoples was put on earth to wait on 'em and work they fields. Colored peoples had no rights to go on down the road, live they own life. They's beat and chained up if they tried to run off and they's sometimes hung. That war was spose to set us free, but we ain't free.

All these years and we still segagated from white peoples here in the South. Ah been told that some us colored peoples went to the North and they free but we not down here. Mah preacher say the day'll come when we not be segagated in the South. Maybe that so, but maybe not while ah is still living."

Toxie paused, glancing over her shoulder.

"Chile, you promise me, when Miss Ionia come in from the yard, you don't say nuthin about eating in the kitchen with me.

Old Toxie need her job. Miss Ionia would give me down the country if she knowed you was a wanting to do such a thing. Might even tell me hit the road. It just won't do, so when suppertime come you go on out to the big table and eat with the white peoples."

I did as Toxie asked, kept quiet and ate at the big table. I thought of her throughout supper. She had never been to school but had given me a life lesson of what living in the South held today and in the future.

That first week of school I spent my afternoons in the kitchen reading "The Black Stallion" to Toxie. During the exciting chapters Toxie would shout out "Law, no!" and when the shipwreck happened she left the stove and stood over me, wringing her hands and saying, "That poor chile and purty black horse in the hands of the Lord now!"

When I tired of reading, Toxie would ask how Daddy was and if any fences had mended at home. I liked and trusted Toxie. I told her about the stereo and songs Daddy listened to over and over, how he rarely spoke to any of us and the fights between him and Mama that left her screaming every night. Toxie looked at me with a sad expression on her face.

"Chile, you be careful. Your daddy got the blue devils."

When I wasn't spending summers on the farm, I spent all my afternoons with Toxie. I never wanted to go home. Along with the madness, crying and screaming, the house was always filled with music. Daddy came home with new records every day. He played them over and over 'til I knew the songs by heart. The words of each new song were like a message.

I no longer know what's real anymore.
In the back of my mind I have opened the door
That leads to the past and the love we once shared.
I keep asking myself, 'What am I doing there?'

I don't remember the day or year that the blue devils came and made my daddy's spirit unclean. It could have been the day our family outings stopped or maybe when he no longer joined us at the table for meals. When the blue devils came, they stayed with Daddy 'til his death.

Looking back, I believe they were always with him and I was just too young to see. In the beginning I never saw him take the drink but knew when it was in him. He'd arrive late at night, and from the room I shared with Little Brother I'd hear the sound of him stumbling and cursing and then Mama crying and screaming.

With each drink the blue devils grew stronger, and now there was always the drink. When Daddy was home, he glared at us, sometimes pointing his finger and saying, "If it wasn't for you." We stayed quiet and out of sight, waiting for him to leave and dreading his return. Mama's screams in the night became more desperate, and in the light of day there were bruises along her arms. Each night brought more madness. When the screams were too much for Little Brother and he began to cry, I'd hide him in the closet and cover him with clothes. Then I'd sit with my back to the closet door, hoping Daddy hadn't heard his cries.

Walking home from school, I could hear the music a block away and gauge Daddy's mood and condition. The blue devils were dancing to Daddy's music now. Hank Williams or George Jones meant he was not quite there yet, just winding up. We had some time and might make it through supper before things went bad. Bluegrass meant he was already there, ready to kick ass, or maybe he already had. I dreaded and hated the sound of those beautiful banjos, fiddles, mandolins and guitars.

There were nights when the screaming stopped and the house fell silent and I'd leave my bed and find Mama on the kitchen floor bloody and unconscious. I could only leave her there, afraid that the slightest sound would wake the blue devils. During that year there were six nights when there was no screaming. Daddy crashed his truck in six separate wrecks that would have killed a sober man, but the blue devils weren't yet finished with him. The six nights he spent in the hospital we slept through the night. With sunrise the day of his release we were prisoners once more.

Children who live a nightmare life have a gift. Their bodies and minds adjust. As with any family structure or schedule, they know what to expect, and it becomes the norm. They feel fear but tuck it away in imaginary boxes in their heads where fear can no longer hurt or frighten them. When I heard the blue devils speak, I lost that gift, no longer able to tuck away my fear. I knew the worst of the nightmares were still to come.

It was three in the morning, and Mama's hand was on my shoulder shaking me awake. I heard Daddy and another man's voice somewhere in the house. She held her finger to her lips signaling me to be quiet. She whispered, "Someone is in the house with your daddy. They are arguing. Your daddy is threatening to kill this man. Get your brother. We have to leave."

I carried Little Brother to the car, and as Mama dressed I went back inside. The voices were louder now; I could hear the sounds of a struggle from the den off the kitchen. I walked softly into the kitchen and tiptoed toward the door leading to the den. There were two plates of half-eaten food on the kitchen table, and an overturned square bottle of amber liquid had drained onto the table and was dripping to the floor. Each drop sounded magnified like the ticking of a large clock.

I reached the door to the den and looked in. There was no one there but Daddy. He was jumping and dodging blows, fighting no one. But two voices were coming from him. One was my daddy's voice. The other filled me with fear. It was the voice of the blue devils.

Otha

That summer, the second week of Larraine and Little Brother's visit, Cordie told me something I already knew. She said Larraine loved horses and thought it would be good for her to have one. I'd took notice of the look on Larraine's face when 'em neighbor boys rode over and let her brush down and sometimes ride their horses. When Larraine was two years old I put her up on the bony back of our old milk cow and led her around the yard while holding her hand to keep her from falling off. Larraine loved it and cried ever time the ride ended. Shoot, riding came as natural as walking to her. Cordie had a way of reading my mind and knew I was thinking we didn't have no money to buy a horse.

Then she told me something I suspected but didn't know for sure. The man down at Fields Grocery told me a week or so back that George had been in there buying cigarettes and beer. Said he almost didn't recognize him, that he was staggering drunk and he couldn't believe George was out driving in such a condition. Cordie told me that Larraine spoke to her about George, said he had the blue devils and she was afraid of him. Cordie reminded me about the fear I had that maybe Larraine was growing a bitterweed heart, saying a horse would give her something to take care of and love and take her away from the misery that was home. Cordie even had a plan on how to get one.

Besides the milk cow we had a young heifer and another calf on the way. Cordie thought maybe we could trade the heifer to one of the neighbors for a horse and that way it wouldn't cost nothing. I put out word and two weeks later Oscar Dunn come over, said he had a young gelding he'd trade for the heifer. He said they called the horse Dynamite and it hadn't been broke yet. I figured any one of 'em boys that rode over now and then to visit could break the gelding for me. I was curious as to why Oscar called the horse Dynamite. Oscar said cause it was a fine, red, dynamite-looking horse and that's how he come up with the name. I made the trade.

Larraine walked with me and Oscar the two miles back to his farm, each of us taking turns leading the heifer. I'd told Oscar not to let on about the trade 'til we got to his house. I wanted it to be a surprise. He played along. We took the heifer down to his barn and there was Dynamite in the barn lot. Just like Oscar said, he was a good-looking red horse with a gold mane, a blaze face and a sleek coat. He was well fed. Larraine went straight to him. While we put the heifer in one of the stables, she climbed up on the fence rail whistling, trying to get him to come closer. Oscar walked over, put his hand on Larraine's shoulder, and called out, "Dynamite. Dynamite, come here, boy. Got someone wants to meet you."

Dynamite came running and stood at the fence letting Larraine rub her hand up and down his blaze.

"Larraine, you like this horse?"

"Yes, sir. I sure do."

"Well, it's a good thing you like him cause Otha just traded that heifer for him."

Larraine looked at me and I nodded yes. She looked back at Oscar. I don't think she believed either one of us. It wasn't 'til I tied the rope to the halter and led him out of the barn lot that she knew it was real. The horse was hers. For the whole two-mile trip home she could hardly walk for talking and looking back to make sure Dynamite was still following behind us. She was going to buy him a bright red bridle and sugar cubes and apples for treats. She musta hugged me around the waist and said thank ya a dozen times.

The first time I tried to switch the halter to a bridle Dynamite reared and fought the bit and damn near got away from me. Me and him fought that way for a week 'til he finally settled down enough to keep the bit in his mouth. He still wasn't no pleasure to lead about, shaking his head back and forth and prone to rearing at any time. I stayed close by when Larraine took him from the stable for walks. Next time 'em neighbor boys rode over I talked 'em into breaking Dynamite. Four of the boys stepped up and we took Dynamite out to a open field. No sooner than one got up on his back that horse threw him. Dynamite threw ever one of 'em. Some of the boys tried twice with the same result. Dynamite was so worked up by then he'd charge 'em afore they could get up off the ground. The last boy he throwed came over to me limping and slapping the dust off his britches.

"Mr. Otha, I broke many a horse but this one here ain't never gone be broke. Don't know how much out of pocket you are with this fine red horse, but you bought yourself a devil."

I was having second thoughts about how Dynamite got his name. Cordie had been as happy as Larraine when she first saw him, saying he was a beautiful horse, but now she had concerns about him being the right horse for a young girl. Cordie was afraid Oscar Dunn had skimmed the truth about Dynamite and we had just been took.

Cordie was right about Oscar Dunn and she was right about Larraine. She was happier than I'd ever seen her. Cordie let her pick the knobby apples from our fruit trees, and Larraine was up at dawn ever morning going with me to the barn carrying a sack full of 'em. She helped me slop the hogs and put out hay and grains for the cows and mules. Then she'd cut up the apples and mix 'em in sweet feed for Dynamite. It had been our routine all that summer, Larraine going into the lot talking to Dynamite while I stood at the fence rail watching. Nothing was different from any other morning, but that one Saturday is seared in my head as to how quick things can go wrong.

Larraine was at the trough pouring in the sweet feed and apples. Dynamite stood behind her like he did at ever feeding. Out of nowhere he reached out and sank his teeth into her shoulder, picked her up off her feet, and tossed her to his right. She hit the dirt hard, landing facedown. I was halfway over the fence rail when he pawed the ground, lowered his head and started in Larraine's direction. Don't know how I moved so fast, but I was in 'tween Dynamite and Larraine afore my mind knowed I'd taken a step. I picked up the feed bucket lying next to Larraine and swung it, hitting Dynamite in the side of his head. He reared and I hit him again, striking at any part of him I could, all the while yelling at the top of my lungs. Cordie heard the commotion and was running toward the barn.

A couple more hits with the feed bucket and Dynamite backed down. I picked Larraine up and carried her out of the lot toward Cordie. We got her in the house. There was blood pouring from her nose, her blouse was ripped away on the right shoulder, and bruises were already showing along her collar bone. Bruises in the shape of that goddamn horse's teeth. Cordie put cool wet rags to her nose and stopped the bleeding. Larraine kept saying she was all right.

Cordie checked her shoulder, legs and arms. "I don't think nothing's broke, but her collar bone might be cracked. I'll wrap her up tight and keep her still for the next couple of weeks. She'll be stove up for a while but she's okay."

I was relieved but mad as hell. Cordie went to the closet, pulled out a sheet, and started ripping it in long pieces to wrap Larraine's shoulder. I went to the gun rack, took my gun down, loaded it, and was on my way out of the house to put a bullet in Dynamite's head. Then I was gonna walk two miles down the road and put the rest of what was in the chamber in Oscar Dunn.

Larraine knew what I was about to do and went hysterical.

"No, Otha! Don't hurt him! It was my fault, all my fault! I'll be more careful next time! I promise! Please!"

Cordie told her not to worry and pulled me, gun in hand, out to the porch.

"Ya think I don't know what ya thinking about doing? I told ya she's gonna be all right. Ya not gonna kill Oscar Dunn and go way for the rest of your life. And ya not gonna kill that horse. Ya shoot that horse and Larraine will never forget it. Wild and crazy as Dynamite is, she loves him. Don't shoot him. Sell him and get her a gentler horse. There's a horse out there somewhere for her. Ya just got to find it."

Cordie took the gun from my hand and went back inside to tend to Larraine. I went down to the barn lot and stood looking at Dynamite, thinking I might mix him up another batch of sweet feed and apples with a little something extra that would put him down by evening. I was damn near about to do it when Cordie called out from the porch saying she needed more water drawed from the well.

Jan Fink

Licking The Salt Block

I knew that by my next summer on the farm Dynamite would be gone. I imagined him somewhere on an island, running free and unbroken for the rest of his life. I wanted the same. I wanted to stow away on a ship going to an island where I could run and play, and live in quiet. But stowing away on ships and living on islands were only stories in the books I read. They weren't real. The stories were made up in the minds of those who wrote them. I was grounded with no place to go.

The bruises along my neck and shoulders had faded to pale blue and yellow by the time I got back home that summer. I didn't share what happened or show my injuries to anyone but Toxie. I told her my dream had come true with my summer with Dynamite. Then I told her how out of nowhere, while I was feeding him, he went crazy. She looked me over and said, "Do go on. You mean tell me a horse pick you up and sail you like a rock?"

"It wasn't his fault, Toxie. He's just an animal. Maybe he was having a bad day."

"Looking at 'em bruises. It seem more like the bad day was yours."

"Otha was going to shoot him, but Cordie talked him out of it."

"Ah tries not disagree with white peoples, but if ah been Miss Cordie ah let Mister Otha shoot that horse dead."

"Cordie said Otha was going to find me another horse. One that's been broke and gentle."

"Ah hope he do. Hope the next one ain't full a mean blood. He gets you nother horse, just you watch and see, chile. Even a blind hog find a acorn now and then. Now ah gonna make us a coconut cake to go with supper while you read the end oh that story about the purty black horse."

I had just finished reading Toxie the last chapter of "The Black Stallion" when Ionia came in from her garden.

"I won't be taking supper tonight, Toxie. I'm tired and going straight to bed."

"Yes, Miss Ionia. Ah leave you a plate case you hungry later."

"No need. Put up the leftovers. I fed the mynah bird but be sure and give old Mac some of the table scraps. I'll see you in the morning."

It was not like Ionia to leave her work in the garden 'til the sun set and more not like her to take to her bed in the afternoon. She pulled off her apron, hung it on the hook near the back door, and went down the hall to her bedroom.

"Chile, you took a good look at Miss Ionia of late? She not eat nuff to keep a baby thriving. And over breakfast last week she says a most 'culiar thing. She say they something in her body. Something that ain't spose to be there. When she not out in that garden she out back with that old iron pot a hers. She builds a fire under it most ever day now and puts water, roots and leaves o' stuff she grows and cooks it down and drinks it. How she drinks it, ah don't know. What she put in that pot smell bad. Real bad."

Ever since Ionia had become a contrary, she had been different for over a year now. Her drinking remedies were nothing new, but I agreed with Toxie that she didn't look good.

At the start of the new school year Mama found religion and joined the Freewill Baptist Church. She took me and Little Brother along to every service, hoping we'd find religion too. The preacher told us Freewill Baptists believed in free grace, free salvation and free will. The church was as contrary as Ionia. I didn't feel free grace as the preacher pounded the pulpit and screamed out his weekly sermon. Salvation was far from free; you really had to work at it. As for free will, I quickly learned not to question the words written in the little Bible they gave me. The Bible was God's word and to question it made you a sinner. They had us memorize Bible verses and to sing a little song at the start of each Sunday school class.

Jesus loves the little children,
All the children of the world.
Red and yellow, black and white,
They are all precious in his sight.
Jesus loves the little children of the world.

I had questions. Where was this Jesus that we were told to rest assured that he would watch over and keep us? He wasn't in my home when the blue devils danced and the screaming began. Where were the red, yellow and black children Jesus loves? They weren't in our church. I didn't take my questions to the preacher or my Sunday school teacher. I took them to Toxie.

"Toxie, do you go to church?"

"Shore ah do."

"Are there any red, yellow and black children in your church?"

"What you going on bout now, chile? Ah ain't never seen no yellah or red chirrens, but we got black chirrens in our church."

"Mama's taking us to church and we don't have any red, yellow or black children coming to our church. The song they taught us says Jesus loves all those children. Do you believe in Jesus? Because I don't think I do. I've never seen him at home or in our church either."

"Ah never knowed a chile that studied on books and things way you do. Ah not be at church if ah didn't believe in Jesus. Jesus not somebody you can see out right. He in your heart and mind. Tween me and you the church don't have nuthin to do with finding Jesus. That something you got to do yourself. It different for everybody. When it happen, it make you want to go to church and sometime it don't. Long as you live a right life you got Jesus in your heart and mind."

"You think maybe you could bring some of the black children from your church and you could all go to Sunday school with me?"

"Oh, chile, that no more let than eating supper here in the kitchen with me. Us colored peoples ain't let in your churches or schools. That what ah been telling you about. We segagated, ain't let to be in 'em places."

What Toxie said made me sad and also made me think. So Jesus loves all the children in his sight as long as they are not together under the same roof of worship.

Freewill Baptist had an after-school Bible camp for two weeks, and Mama was quick to sign me and Little Brother up. The bus picked us up at four in the afternoon and brought us home at seven in the evening. The bus driver would start honking the horn when he turned onto our street. He didn't like to be kept waiting, smelled like the cigarettes Daddy smoked, and always yelled out "Praise God!" when he opened and closed the bus door.

On the last day of Bible study at camp our teacher asked the ten members of my class to kneel with her in prayer. She told us we were sinners, our hearts were wrong, we were already condemned and could not save ourselves. She took the Bible in her hand, flipping the pages 'til she found the passage she was looking for. Then she read aloud:

"You must trust the Lord Jesus to be saved. Now repeat after me: For whosoever shall call upon the name of the Lord shall be saved."

Like sheep all ten of us did as this adult told us to. As I repeated her words I knew she had pulled off a mass production of salvation. Our baptisms were scheduled for the coming Sunday. The preacher and members of the church called it a miracle and praised our teacher. They believed she had been truly blessed by the Lord to bring her entire class to the arms of Jesus.

I did not believe that I was a sinner with a wrong heart and already condemned. I told this to Mama. She said the baptismal gown was already bought and I would not embarrass her in front of the whole congregation by renouncing my salvation.

Sunday came, the baptismal tank was filled with tepid water, and I was crying. I cried in the dressing room and in line waiting for my salvation dunk and cried even harder when the preacher put me beneath the water. When my baptism was done, the congregation shook my hand, gave me a bookmark for my little Bible, and told me my tears were a true sign of being filled with Jesus' spirit.

But Jesus was not there. I was not saved.

Mama put all her energy into the church and the preacher's sermons. She was sure Jesus would soon deliver us from the evil that the blue devils had brought to our home. She told me that my summer on the farm would be cut short by two weeks of vacation Bible school. I didn't want to go. Mama said now that I was saved I had to go. I tried to tell her I wasn't saved because to be saved from sin you had to sin, and I wasn't really sure what sin was. She told me I was going, like it or not, and that Jesus was coming and all our troubles would be over. I hoped Mama was right but at the same time wondered what was taking Jesus so long. Mama, Little Brother and I had been in church for every service, and the blue devils were still raging at home. If anything they were stronger. I saw the blue devils every day, but not once did I see Jesus. Toxie said you couldn't see Jesus, but you felt him in your heart and mind. Either way, I didn't think Jesus was coming to help us.

Otha was waiting on the front porch when Mama dropped me off for the summer. He was all excited. He had got one hundred and fifty dollars for Dynamite, and we were going horse hunting. We hitched a ride to the edge of town and then walked the last mile to the stockyards. It was a big old rickety building that looked like it'd fall in if you bumped into a wall. The inside was row after row of open stalls with a single fence rail across the front. A path strewn with hay ran the length of the building from the front to the rear. It was dark, damp, heavy with the smell of urine and manure and the sounds of stamping hooves and neighing from the stalls.

There were colts and fillies, fat quarter horses and old worn-out swayback mares with every rib showing. Stall after stall there was more of the same 'til we reached the last stall on the left rear wall. There he was, like he'd stepped right off the pages of my book. The big black stallion's halter was chained to a large hook screwed into the ceiling of his stall. The short length of chain held his head up high allowing him no movement other than constant turning in circles. A couple of other men joined me and Otha. They tapped on the fence rail and whistled, trying to get the stallion's attention. The stallion's pace quickened as he turned round and round with eyes wide, nostrils flared and his neighing as shrill as a human screaming.

One of the men at the stall with us said, "Only a fool would buy this one. That horse gonna kill somebody." The man was probably right, but I can still see that stallion. Such a beautiful, wild, sad creature.

There was a neighbor man called Sullivan who shoed horses for a living. Otha talked to him and Sullivan did know of a horse belonging to a man in town. He'd shoed the man's horses for years and knew their temperaments. He said the mare was a Tennessee Walker that had been used as a racking horse. She was seven years old and retired from racking, so the man might be willing to sell her. Sullivan picked us up early the next morning. I was nervous and asking questions all the way to town. Sullivan said she was solid black with a white blaze down her face and called Velvet after the movie *National Velvet*. She was a gentle horse that didn't give him any trouble when he put shoes on her, and she'd never been known to kick or bite.

On the outskirts of town Sullivan turned down a long lane that was lined with big oaks and white wood fences marking pastures as far as you could see on both sides. Horses of all sizes and colors grazed in the tall grass, some looking up at us from behind the fence rails as we rumbled along in Sullivan's old truck. At the end of the lane was one of the biggest houses I'd ever seen. It was a tall two-story, with porches upstairs and down that ran the length of the house. Across the front were white columns so big you could hide behind them. To the right and back of the house was a barn nearly as big as the house itself. To the left were fields of corn and a silo that looked down on all the other buildings. Sullivan said it was an old plantation that had been in the man's family for a long time.

Two big, gray, ghostly-looking dogs met us out front and circled the truck, barking to announce our arrival. We stayed in the truck 'til the man came out and put up his dogs. He took us down to the barn and Velvet's stall. His barn was nothing like the stockyard barn we'd gone to the day before. It was nice and clean and even had electric lighting.

Velvet was beautiful, standing quietly as he bridled her and led her from the stall. He offered to saddle her, but I told him I was used to riding bareback. I had to stand on a feed bucket and hold to her mane to pull myself onto her back. Otha took the reins from me and led her around the yard. I knew he was thinking about Dynamite and wanted to see what Velvet would do before he let me ride alone. After a couple of trips around the yard he stopped and ran his hand under Velvet's stomach, across her hindquarters and down her back legs. She didn't move an inch, just stood quiet.

Otha handed me the reins, and I rode about as the men struck a deal. Velvet could be bought but her asking price was two hundred dollars. Fifty more than Otha had to spend. After a lot of talking Sullivan offered to do fifty dollars' worth of free shoeing for the owner if Otha signed a promise to pay him back when the next cotton crop was taken to the gin. The man agreed to the arrangement and even offered the loan of one of his horse trailers to get Velvet home to the farm.

The rest of that summer I was up at dawn and riding the trails deep into the woodland 'til sunset. When I was on Velvet's back I was happy and free, wanting summer to go on forever. Once a week I rode her farther than the forty acres that was Cordie and Otha's farm. Otha had taken me to the remains of the old homestead years earlier. The hundred acres it sat on now belonged to a timber company. There was nothing left of

Duck John's place but the fieldstone chimney standing tall like the statues of Easter Island, holding untold stories about the family that once lived there. There was a pond on the property that Otha said had never been known to dry up even in the worst summer droughts. Otha thought old Duck John had made a pact with the devil to have water all year round while other folks' wells and ponds dried up. To prove his point he showed me the devil's snuff that lay in clumps around the pond. If you stepped on it, the snuff would burst into the air and cover your shoes and clothing.

It was my favorite place to go. As Velvet grazed and drank from the pond, I'd sit and imagine old Duck John somewhere in the woodland making his deal with the devil.

That same summer I was witness to my first tornado. On our summer visits I slept with Cordie and Little Brother slept with Otha. Cordie kept her bedroom window open winter and summer to gauge the weather and hear the sounds coming from the yard chickens and livestock in the barn. The slightest call or unusual movements from them would send her out of bed to Otha's room, warning him that a fox, coyote, snakes, or maybe an unwelcome human had breached the farm. On those nights Otha would take up a lantern and gun and walk his farm 'til he found the interloper. There were many nights when he found a fox or coyote with one of Cordie's prize hens still in its mouth or a rattler in the barn lot or stable too near the livestock.

The day the tornado came Cordie left our bed at one that morning. I lingered in bed waiting for the sound of Otha leaving the house to patrol his farm. All was quiet other than the call of a whippoorwill deep in the woodland and the sound of Cordie's footsteps in the kitchen. I got up and found her stacking kindling in the woodstove. She lit another lantern and asked me to go to the well and draw a bucket of water for coffee. Then she began taking the iron skillets down from the nails along the wall. When the coffee, biscuits and golden yolk eggs were almost done, she called Otha and Little Brother to breakfast.

"Cordie, what ya doing up so early this morning?"

"The air ain't right, Otha. We need to get to the fields soon as the sun is up."

Little Brother looked across the table to Otha and broke into song.

"The air ain't right, the air ain't right. Going to the fields cause the air ain't right."

"Hush, boy. And listen up to what ya grandmama's telling us. Ya think a storm a-coming, Cordie?"

"May be. Not sure, but ever bone in my body been talking to me since midnight. Somethings coming. Something bad. I think the kids ought to go to the fields with us and stay close by."

With the first peek of sunlight we went to the fields, walking up and down the rows behind Cordie and Otha as they hoed away the weeds among their vegetables. When noon came Cordie pulled tomatoes from the vine and dug up radishes, wiping them clean with her apron, then took the little pouch of salt that she carried in her apron pocket and dusted them white. We sat between the rows and ate, the sun on our backs.

At three o'clock Cordie stopped along a row and stood leaning on her hoe looking up at the sky.

"Otha, ya hear that?" Otha turned and looked toward the woodland.

"Don't hear nothing, Cordie."

"That's just it. Ain't a sound or a bird in sight. The air done turned close and thick. We need to get back to the house and get ready."

The wind came suddenly whistling through the pines at the edge of the woodland. The rain began before we cleared the fields. Cordie and Otha put me and Little Brother between them, held our hands, and told us to run. The wind pushed the rain into our faces and thunder began to rumble in the distance. We reached the storm pit and the rain turned to hail. Small spits of ice quickly became quarter-size. Cordie pushed me and Little Brother to the ground, took off her apron and covered us.

"Stay here with your brother. I'm going for the lanterns."

I put my arms around Little Brother and held him tight. I watched from beneath the apron as Otha entered the storm pit with his hoe and chased out three big rat snakes. As the hail pelted them, they hissed and raced across the yard. Cordie came back with the lanterns and took us into the blackness of the dark, dirt pit. When the lanterns were lit, Otha was not there with us.

"Cordie! Where's Otha?"

"Gone to let the stock out of the barn. He'll be back."

"No! He can't put Velvet out in the storm!"

"Larraine, it got to be done!"

I ran from the pit toward the barn. Otha had already taken Velvet, the mules and cows from their stables and was waving his arms and shouting, herding them out of the lot gate. The wind had increased, sending the hail flying flat, its force snapping pines. Velvet and the mules were running into the woodland, but the cows lingered outside the lot, their heads lowered.

I began to run after Velvet, calling her, my voice lost in the wind. Otha caught me around the waist, threw me over his shoulder, and ran to the pit, me kicking and pounding him with my fists all the way. Once inside he closed the pit door and sat me down next to Cordie.

"Why did you do that, Otha? How could you put her out in the storm?"

"Listen to me, Larraine. The woodland is the best place your Velvet can be right now. Animals have a way a knowing the safe place to be. If I left her and my mules and cows in that barn and the storm took it down on 'em how you think I'd feel leaving 'em trapped that away to die? She gone be all right."

Cordie put her arm around me, took my hand, and patted it. "Ya understand, don't ya? Otha done what he had to do. He couldn't leave 'em animals trapped."

I could barely hear Cordie. The thunder was right above us now, booming nonstop. Little Brother began to cry, calling out to me.

"Rainie! Is that Daddy coming? Hurry! Take me to the closet!"

Cordie pulled him into her lap and covered his ears with her hands. "Hush, now. That's not your daddy. It just a bad old storm. We gonna stay right here 'til it passes. We gonna be fine."

Then there came a sudden stillness. That day I learned that the wind, thunder, rain and hail had only been the prelude. The quiet stillness that followed was the true announcer of all Alabama tornadoes. Cordie and Otha pushed me and Little Brother low, our faces against the damp earth floor of the pit, and covered us with their bodies. The ground beneath us trembled, the sound of more trees snapping accompanied by a low growl that was gaining speed, the growl becoming a roar and with it heavy rain. It stalled over the storm pit, roaring, rattling the wooden door and bringing chunks of dirt down from the ceiling that covered and choked us. Water began to trickle in beneath the door and then rush in like the run-off of a swollen creek. The twister stayed there above us, in no hurry to relinquish its power and move on. It seemed an eternity before it left as quickly as it came.

We waited, unsure, afraid to move. When the water ceased running into the pit, Otha tried to open the door. The heavy rain had deposited a thick wall of mud on the other side. He and Cordie put their shoulders to the door and pushed while reaching around it to clear away the mud. We stood outside, wet and muddy, looking up at sunshine and blue skies. It was as if nothing had happened and the tornado had never visited, but Mother Nature is a trickster. It was only 'til our eyes recovered focus from the darkness of the pit to sunshine that we knew.

Trees in the yard lay splintered like kindling. The outhouse and chicken coop were gone, leaving no trace of their existence. Otha had not had time to free the hogs from their pen. The pine boards along one wall were broken and lying in the mud. They had trampled the enclosure to flee the storm. There were chickens, some dead and others dying, strewn about the rain-soaked ground like wet stuffed animals, but no sign of Velvet, the mules, hogs or cows.

The barn leaned dangerously to the right; the foot of the tornado had done its best to push it to the ground. I knew then that Otha had done the right thing by releasing Velvet. I felt guilty about my mistrust, but not a word passed between any of us. We stood shivering in the bright sunshine looking toward the farmhouse and smokehouse. They were still standing, completely untouched.

We went through the rest of the afternoon in a daze. Otha picked up the injured and dying chickens, wrung their necks, plucked their feathers, and prepared them for the big pot of water Cordie had heating on the woodstove. Then he drew more water from the well, filling up the washtubs so we could bathe and get into dry clothes. By early afternoon neighbor men began to arrive. They helped Otha clear the yard of debris and shared stories of their damage and news of others in the community. The Barnett family five miles east had lost everything. Two miles down the road, Oscar Dunn's wife had been killed when the wind took down a large oak, sending it through the roof of the kitchen as she cooked. Oscar's barn and all his livestock inside had met the same fate by the same wind.

They told of limbs and pieces of tin roofing being forced through large pines, leaving the tree standing, pine needles and pine cones untouched. Some spoke of the sound of the tornado, comparing it to the devil arriving on a freight train from hell. The afternoon was filled with such stories. Men worked, shaking their heads and thanking God that their home and family had been spared and escaped the worst of it. Before they moved on to help the next neighbor in need, Cordie served them cool well water, cornbread and a stew made from the chickens the tornado had thrown and tossed about a few hours earlier.

As the men were leaving, I listened while they made plans with Otha to come back in the next few weeks to help him take down the leaning barn. All my thoughts were of Velvet. I only had another week and a half left of my summer visit. We had to find her or I would refuse to leave the farm, even if I had to hide in the woodland.

Before sunset Otha and I went down to the pasture, both of us calling out as he beat the feed bucket with his hands, hoping to draw Velvet and the livestock from the woodland. Cordie's young milk cow, Li'l Belle, was the first to heed, running through the brush and downed trees, her bell bouncing on her neck, loudly ringing. Big Frank, Otha's youngest plow mule, came next. Otha emptied some of the feed on the ground and as they ate we continued to call, but only Li'l Belle and Big Frank had come as night fell.

Early the next morning Otha and I went deep into the woodland looking and calling out to the missing. Five acres in we found Ol' Belle. Faithful Ol' Belle whose milk had nourished me as an infant when my mother's milk could not and through the years provided our table with butter and buttermilk. The tornado had wrapped her around the base of a large oak, breaking her back. We stood in silence, looking down at her. She almost seemed to be asleep, snuggled against the oak. I reached out and touched her, but she was cold and stiff, life gone.

"Otha, should we bury her?"

"Larraine, me and ya can't bury her. It'd take a half dozen strong men, digging for days to put Ol' Belle in the ground. We gonna have to leave her to nature. Nature takes care of these things. We need to go on and see if we can find some of the living."

Another acre away we found Otha's small, older plow mule, Maud. She was standing in brush up to her belly with scratches and cuts covering most of her body. The worst cut was above her left eye. We cleared the brush away and Otha put the rope he'd brought along around her neck. He checked her legs and then her eye. Otha and Maud had battled their way across many a field from sun-up to sundown, Otha often resorting to cussing the stubborn mule, but that day he put his arms around her neck and spoke softly to her.

"Ya gonna be all right, Maud, old gal. That damn tornado done took your eye, but ya can still pull the plow. Me and ya got many more rows to make."

I remained in the woodland as Otha took Maud back home to clean and care for her injuries. I went back over the six acres we had searched and then deeper into the woodland, calling out to Velvet, but there was no sign of her. I gave up at dusk, Cordie's dinner bell calling me home. We took dinner on the front porch that night, listening to the birds call from the woodland. Cordie and Otha were quiet. I knew they were worried about the losses.

"Cordie, I'm sorry about Ol' Belle. I know you'll miss her."

"I will miss her, Larraine. She was the best milk cow I ever owned. But she give me Li'l Belle, so we gone have milk, butter and buttermilk. She done well by me. Ya got to think on the good. Same with Velvet. Ya got to think on the good. I just know Velvet gone come back to ya. She's just out there somewhere scared. Everything gonna be okay."

Otha agreed with Cordie. "Your grandmama's right. Velvet coming back. Wait and see. When ya was in the woodland, did ya see any a my hogs?"

"No, sir."

"Yeah, just as I figured. When hogs get loose in the woodland they go back to being wild. Don't need no human feeding 'em. We probably won't never see a one of 'em hogs again. That gonna make for a lean winter far as meat go. I hope least one of 'em shows back up. They'll be enough wood when we take down the barn to build another chicken coop, an outhouse and a lean-to for the livestock."

Cordie smiled and patted Otha on the back. "Well, first thing ya need to build is the chicken coop. While ya and Larraine was in the woodland, Pearl and Lee Barnett come by. They staying with their daughter now 'til they can rebuild. They said their daughter got more Banty hens and roosters than she needs, so they gone bring us some. We could pen 'em up 'til ya get the coop built. Banties are small but they good layers. We'll have eggs for breakfast and chickens for dinner. Think on the good, Otha."

I took Cordie's lead and tried to think on the good. It was two days later while I was in the pasture with Otha for the morning feeding that Velvet emerged from the woodland. She was skittish and muddy, her mane and tail full of cockleburs but not a mark on her. I spent the remainder of my summer visit taking her to the creek to wash away the mud and combing and cutting the cockleburs from her beautiful mane and tail.

Otha thought it best that I didn't ride her right away but let her settle back into routine. I was good with that. All that mattered was she was back. I could leave the farm knowing she was safe and unharmed.

Vacation Bible school was pretty much the same as after school Bible camp. We learned verses from the Bible and were told to be good children. Little Brother never paid attention or learned his verses. His favorite part of the whole experience was refreshment time. He went home every day with his mouth and clothes covered with cookie crumbs and grape Kool-Aid stains. I missed Velvet, hated being back home and hated vacation Bible school.

Mama was wearing long sleeves even in summer to hide the bruises along her arms. The music from Daddy's stereo and the fights between him and Mama played out every night. Daddy took up hunting. He bought two coon dogs and rifles and shotguns. During the fall hunting season we were spared the crazy nights when Daddy loaded up his hounds and took to the woodland with his friends.

Christmas of that year the church decided to do a live nativity scene. One of the church members could supply sheep and a cow, but no one had a donkey, so I volunteered Velvet. She didn't look the part, but the preacher was set on doing the nativity scene and arranged for a trailer to pick her up. He filled the parsonage carport with hay and ran a heavy chain across the front to tether Velvet to. Velvet was a perfect lady throughout the first performance. That night at home when the first fight and screaming began I thought of Velvet. I took a flashlight and my heavy coat from the hall closet and walked the six blocks to the parsonage. She was happy to see me, nudging my hands with her soft muzzle. I settled into the hay for the night with her, sure that I wouldn't be missed at home.

I was drifting into sleep when the flicker of a flashlight came up the driveway. I was afraid the preacher had heard me talking to Velvet. I moved to the back of the carport and covered myself with hay.

"Chile, you in there?"

"Toxie?"

"Ah knowed you be here. Ah knowed you not think bout bringing a blanket or nuthin. Ah lives just down the road a ways and sides, ah ain't seen your new horse yet."

Toxie spread out the blanket she had tucked under her arm. She took the pillow case that was tied to her belt and pulled out biscuits wrapped in small cut pieces of flour sack and laid them on the blanket. We sat on the blanket watching Velvet and shared one of the biscuits that she'd smeared inside with butter and honey.

"Mister Otha shore done right by you. She bout the purtiest animal ah ever seen. She look as good as that black stallion in your book. Ah thinks even Jesus would say she much more easy on the aahs than a donkey. Ah can tell her ain't got no mean blood in her." Toxie reached back into the pillow case and pulled out a handful of carrots.

"Ah ain't got no apple trees, but ah thinks horses eats carrots. Ah brought these from my garden, case Miss Velvet want a snack later."

"You can give her one now."

"Law, no. Ah scares that horse."

"No, you won't. Go ahead. She doesn't bite."

Toxie wouldn't get too close. She leaned toward Velvet and held the carrot out at arm's length. She held the carrot 'til Velvet's teeth got close and then dropped it in the hay.

"Old Toxie got to go. Ah be back morrow night, and ah'm bring you mo' biscuits and carrots for Miss Velvet. Be safe, chile. Don't let that horse step on you in the night."

The horse trailer was brought back the day after the last nativity scene. Velvet refused to go into it. Each time we tried to lead her in, she balked. The preacher asked me to get up in the window of the trailer, hold the rope and call to her, coaxing her in. It was working 'til she was halfway in and then changed her mind. She backed out so quickly she pulled me through the trailer window. I hit the floor of the trailer facedown, still holding the rope. She dragged me through the trailer and down the ramp. My elbows and knees were bloody, the skin rubbed right off of them. My hands were the same where the rope burned through my palms and fingers. A vet was called and gave Velvet a mild tranquilizer. It took another hour before she walked quietly into the trailer. Toxie later said Velvet was a smart horse and just wanted to stay in town with me and get some more of her garden carrots every night.

I made the trip to the farm with Velvet. I sat in front of the fire as Cordie cleaned up my knees, elbows, and hands and put salve on them. I wanted to stay right there with Cordie, Otha and Velvet, but I had to go home for Christmas.

On Christmas Eve the stereo played all day. No "Joy to the World" or "Silent Night" but Hank Williams singing cheating songs and George Jones twanging out "Blue Must Be the Color of the Blues." I didn't believe in Santa Claus anymore. I knew it was Daddy who bought the gifts and put them under the tree. By six that night the music had changed to bluegrass, and I knew Daddy was on his way.

I could hear him late into the night sometimes singing along with the bluegrass, laughing and cussing and then the sound of things breaking. At first light Little Brother woke me, tugging at my hand, ready to see what Santa had brought while we slept. We hurried down the hall and to the living room. The Christmas tree lay on its side, ornaments broken and strewn about the room. Most of the gifts were unwrapped, some of them under the fallen tree and others against the wall.

The bicycle Little Brother had put on his Santa list was halfway put together, its front wheel and fender missing. Daddy was on his back, passed out on top of a list of instructions to build the bicycle. The missing front wheel was lying across his stomach, the fender hooked over his right arm.

A half bottle of whiskey was sitting next to the fallen tree. Cigarette ashes were scattered over the floor like fake snow. The cigarette in Daddy's left hand had fallen and burned itself out, leaving a black hole in the hardwood floor, a black hole burned in forever, leaving its mark for us to see each holiday, reminding us of Christmas past. I took Little Brother back to our room to wait 'til Daddy was up and had left the house.

TWO

Mama lost religion as quickly as she'd found it. She didn't give any reason. I thought maybe she got tired of waiting for Jesus or maybe it was because she now had bruises on her face that she couldn't hide. Mama replaced the church with movie magazines. She went to the Piggly Wiggly once a week and bought one of every publication from the magazine rack. She'd come home with an arm full and spend hours studying all the photos and reading every article. She started scrapbooks of photos of her favorite movie stars. She carefully cut, arranged and pasted the photos down with Elmer's glue on the pages of the scrapbooks. She knew everything about Liz Taylor, Marilyn Monroe, Doris Day and Debbie Reynolds. She talked about them as if they were her close friends. When Eddie Fisher left Debbie Reynolds for Liz Taylor, Mama had a complete come-apart and cried for a week.

While Mama lived with her friends in Hollywood, Daddy lived with his friends in bars and in the woodland hunting. Little Brother and I lived for the weekends and summers on the farm. Ionia's health was rapidly spiraling downward. During the last few months she had become so thin, she looked as if half of her had been carved away. I spent my afternoons in the kitchen with Toxie. Ionia rarely left her bed. She was so tired and weak, there were days when she couldn't lift her head to sip the broth Toxie brought her, but she still refused to consult with a doctor.

Toxie was real worried and said she could see bad days coming. "Miss Ionia worse ever day. She not able to go out and cook up her remedies no mo'. She tell me what leaves and roots to pull up out in the yard and she just eat 'em down raw. Theys ain't doing her no good. She knowed months ago they was something in her body not spose to be there. Chile, your grandmama got the cancer in her."

"What's cancer?"

"Cancer something that come in to you real quiet. You don't know you got it 'til it make its bed. Then it eats you up a little ever day 'til you nuthin but dust. Miss Ionia not long for this life. We got to do all we can for her. She worry about the weeds in her flower beds. You want to help old Toxie do some weed pulling?"

Toxie and I spent two afternoons chasing the peacocks out of their favorite hiding places among the flower beds and pulling out all the weeds and taking them to the street. We went to Ionia's bedside and told her not to worry, that the weeds were gone and her flowers were beautiful. She patted each of our hands and thanked us. Back in the kitchen big tears rolled down Toxie's cheek. She blotted them away with her apron and got busy making the evening meal.

I didn't understand cancer. It was hard to imagine that something could come inside your body and turn you to dust. If Ionia turned to dust, she would no longer be with us. It troubled me. I went to her bedside each afternoon for short visits. Most days she slept. Some days she sat up in bed, her eyes wide, staring at things and talking to people I could not see.

One afternoon she had a gift for me. It was a soft stuffed animal. A basset hound with long floppy ears and sad eyes stitched forever in its face that no amount of love or holding could take away. She'd had someone buy one for me and one for her. She told me that we could talk to each other always by whispering our messages into the ears of our basset hounds. Whenever I was sad or troubled, I could let her know. She took my hand and said, "Always remember I taught you to fly. It's my fault that he does the bad things he does. I let them put it in his head."

"Put what in whose head?"

"The metal plate. It's my fault. I let them put the metal plate in your daddy's head."

They were the last words Ionia spoke to me. She closed her eyes, drifted into sleep, and slumbered 'til five days before Christmas when the cancer took her.

A long black hearse brought her home. Daddy started drinking early morning. He lingered on the front lawn smoking and occasionally nodding at the early mourners awaiting Ionia's viewing. The casket was placed in the parlor. The room was filled with so many fresh flowers, a window had to be raised to allow the sweet scent more space.

The men from the hearse opened the casket. Ionia was not dust. She was inside and looked as though she was sleeping in her garden surrounded by her own flowers. Through the open parlor window I could hear the peacocks in the yard. They screamed and chased each new mourner across the lawn as they arrived for the viewing.

Toxie made cakes and urns of coffee and set the big table in the dining room with Ionia's best china. Mama, Little Brother, and I sat on the stiff gold velvet chairs, this time not covered with towels. We said hello and thank you as people passed through shaking our hands and sometimes hugging us, leaving wet patches of their tears on our cheeks. Grandfather Joe wandered about the room smoking his pipe, never looking at the casket or us. He talked to the mourners about his new investment plans and what a grand day it turned out to be far as weather goes. The smoke from his pipe mingled with the flowers, giving them a sick bittersweet scent that tortured eyes and noses.

The mynah bird cage was covered and taken from the parlor after startling mourners by calling out in Ionia's voice. Old Mac slept beneath the casket. When the viewing was done and the hearse returned to carry Ionia to the cemetery, Old Mac wouldn't let them near her. He stood his ground in front of the casket, bristled and growling, biting anyone who came close to Ionia. It took two men to subdue him. They covered his head with a pillow case, carried him to the bathroom and locked him in. His howls were almost human and mixed with the screams of the peacocks and the crying of mourners as Ionia was taken away.

At the cemetery we sat in uncomfortable folding chairs close enough to reach out and touch Ionia's casket. The casket was suspended over a hole in the ground by sturdy round bars and the ground around it draped in deep blue velvet material. I looked for Toxie in the crowd of mourners but found her standing alone at the edge of the road outside the cemetery fence. I ran to her and took her hand, begging her to come and sit with us near the casket. This was my first funeral and I was afraid and crying.

"Toxie, what's the hole for?"

"Chile, Miss Ionia taking to the ground today. That what happen when we leave dis earth; we go back to it. Don't cry, it a good thing. Your grandmama loved dis earth. Always remember, anything you put in the ground is a good thing, cept for 'em evil peoples in the world. The earth too good for 'em. Go on back now and say bye to Miss Ionia."

When they lowered Ionia and the casket into the ground, I thought of her poking her finger into the rows of rich earth in her garden and dropping in the seeds. I hoped she was happy going back to the earth she tended and loved so.

When the bathroom door was opened, Old Mac went to the spot where the casket had been. For a week he slept there, refusing food or water. Toxie took him out to the yard, hoping she could get him to eat outside. He ignored the food, had no interest in eating. He walked the garden paths in and around the flower beds, whining with his nose to the ground, searching for Ionia. We found him two weeks later in one of the hibiscus beds, his body stiff and frozen to the winter ground.

Toxie said he'd joined Miss Ionia and was now walking new paths with her.

When Ionia and old Mac took to the ground, my whole world was turned upside down. The earth left, becoming the sky. The sky came down with no solid footing and darkness that lingered. Daddy no longer answered to anyone. His friends now came to the house every night and played their forbidden games of dominos, drinking and listening to the music that had become a constant in our home. Mama retreated to her star magazine friends, rarely leaving her room, no longer caring.

Something was happening to me. My chest was growing and sore. I thought of Ionia and hoped I didn't have the cancer. I told Toxie and she laughed. She cupped her chest in both hands.

"Law, chile. That a part of coming a woman. You see these big breasts ah's got. That what being a woman is. You growing up. All womens got breasts. Nuthin to be fraid of. You not got the cancer. That just the way God make womenfolks."

Daddy and his friends noticed the change in my body. After an afternoon of drinking, Daddy called me over and ran his hand up under my shirt.

"Look here. Larraine's getting knobs. You know what that means!"

They laughed like it was the funniest thing they'd ever heard. I hated them all. If this was what being a woman was about, I wanted nothing to do with it. I took rags from the rag bin in the garage and tied down my chest as tightly as I could. I kept the binding on every waking hour and even as I slept. Within weeks I began having pain in the left side of my chest. When I removed the binding, the area around my left nipple was swollen and bright red. I took a new rag and bound my chest down tighter. It only made the pain worse and, days later, blood and pus began soaking through the rags. I cleaned the discharge and changed the rags every day, but when the fever came, I had no choice but to show Mama.

I didn't tell her about the rags or about Daddy. She was just as afraid of him as I was. Things were already bad enough between all of us and to tell her might make things worse. She took me to the doctor. He cut a small hole, drained the area and put me on medication. The doctor told Mama that as soon as the area healed I should be in training bras, so she stopped on the way home and bought three. So like it or not, I was to be a woman.

Toxie's premonition was right. The bad days kept coming. Toxie did her best to keep up the house and tend the flower beds as Ionia had done. In less than a year my Grandfather Joe brought home a new wife. She didn't like Toxie and thought she was unpleasant to look at. My heart splintered the day she told Toxie she was no longer needed. I had grown to love her so. Toxie was my friend, my confidant and teacher. I begged Grandfather Joe to let Toxie stay, but he sat silent, puffing his pipe. I pleaded with Toxie to come back and visit or tell me where she lived, and I'd come see her.

"Toxie, I can't lose you. I love you."

"Chile. You stop fretting bout mah leaving. From the day you born, life gonna take something from you. But everything that happens to you or you do in your life means something. Don't never forget that. It best for the heart we not see one nother again. You got growing up to do and a good new life to find. You keep studying on 'em books you like so. Ah gone miss you too and I love you. Don't forget old Toxie."

She walked down the street, looking back every few yards, waving and smiling, calling out, "Law, Law! Don't forget old Toxie."

With her leaving, Ionia's flower beds went untended. The peacocks were caught, put in cages and sold. Then the new wife called in a landscaper and ordered him to take down every tree and dig up every plant on the property. Ionia's garden was bulldozed and pushed to the edge of the street. Neighbors came and picked through the mound for cuttings and bulbs for their gardens. Little Brother and I made forts among the limbs and brush. We sat along the downed branches of the fruit trees, eating the fruit that was quickly spoiling in the sun. Two days later the trash truck came and took the pile. Ionia's garden was gone for good.

With Ionia's passing, Mama stripped the floral wallpaper throughout our house and painted the walls white. The mynah bird was the last to go. Grandfather Joe said his new wife couldn't bear to hear Ionia's voice coming from that bird. Once the bird was gone there would be no trace or evidence that Ionia ever existed on that piece of land. I got to say my good-byes before the cage was loaded into Grandfather Joe's station wagon. I went to the cage and said, "Hi, mynah, this is Larraine. I'll miss you."

Mynah skittered along his perch towards me and called out in Ionia's voice, "I will teach you to fly. I will teach you to fly."

THREE

I opened up my head today just to look inside.
Never did I expect to see
What was staring back at me.
No nuts or bolts or turning wheels,
Nor tissues as medical books all show;
Just a small dark space, and sitting there was another me.
Eye to eye I challenged,
Come out, let's have a chat.
It's not allowed, a small voice cried from deep within the dark,
For I am here to keep you there.
I thought to reach inside and crush it,
Remove it from my head.
Then the small voice spoke softly, saying,
But who of us would be dead?

I was glad there was another me. I had a better chance of surviving childhood. The other me inside my head shared the fear and anxiety and kept me in check. Without the soft voice constantly reminding me of who of us would be dead, I am sure I could have become a natural-born killer. When other girls' thoughts were of new dresses and summer sandals, I thought about murder and already had a list. Daddy and the blue devils were at the top of it.

Daddy called me out to the backyard. Next to the dog pen where he kept his hounds, there were a half dozen empty whiskey bottles lined up along a slope in the lawn. Daddy was standing next to them with a .22 caliber rifle in one hand and a pint bottle of whiskey in the other. He turned the bottle up and took a long drink. Then he beat the butt of the rifle on the ground.

"You like running around shooting off that little cap gun of yours, playing cowboys and Indians? Well let's see what you can do with the real thing."

Leaning on the rifle, he brought the pint to his lips and drained it, then stood the empty next to the others in the grass. He staggered toward me, his foot hitting a low patch in the lawn, almost falling.

"God dammit!"

He spit on the ground, regained his footing and used the rifle as a walking stick 'til he reached me. He took me by the arm and led me several yards across the lawn. He put the rifle in my hand and pointed to the bottles standing at attention, waiting silently in line for the firing squad.

"Here go. I just wounded them for you. Now you kill them. See if you can kill them all."

The first shot sent the hounds into frenzy. They howled and jumped at the chain link fence, excited and ready to hunt. For a first-time shooter I was remarkably good. When the shells were all spent, I'd managed to kill them all. I turned from the targets and handed the rifle back to Daddy. Then a most unusual thing happened. He stood there quiet, holding the rifle, looking down at me. He'd had a lot of the drink today, but now he seemed almost sober. It was like the blue devils had just up and left him with no warning. He reached out, grabbed my shoulder and shook me a little too roughly.

"Sumbitch! Larraine, you got the eye!"

This unusual state of Daddy's mind was to last four months. There was always the drink and he was never completely sober but for that brief time the blue devils had quit raging. Daddy didn't glare at me so much, and on trips to the store when we ran into neighbors or friends, he'd put his hand on my shoulder and brag.

"See this girl here? I got me an Annie Oakley. Never seen a female shoot like she can."

Throughout the last days of that summer, Daddy would set up the whisky bottles along the slope in the yard and we'd have target practice. His friends would come and sit alongside Daddy in sagging lawn chairs, drinking and cheering as I raised the rifle and took the shot. It is sad to say that during those months I still hated and feared my Daddy, but I took some unsettling comfort in his being so proud of me.

In early fall he began taking me along on hunting trips with his friends. They were late-night excursions deep into the woodland along abandoned logging roads, the truckbed loaded with hounds, rifles and whiskey. When we reached the right spot, the hounds were turned out into the woodland, running and barking on the scent. We waited by the truck 'til their voices changed from short choppy barks to longer, higher, more frantic howls, meaning they had treed. That was our cue to take up the rifles and carbide lamps and follow their voices to where they held a coon, sometimes two, clinging to the high branches.

The hounds knew their job well. They remained at the base of the tree, voices sounding 'til we arrived for the kill. When we reached the tall pine, there were two wild-eyed coons at the top. Daddy called back the hounds.

"Still! Still!"

His friend stepped forward, took the first shot and missed. Daddy laughed. The guy took a second shot. Missed again.

"You crazy drunk sumbitch. You couldn't hit the base of that tree if you were standing three feet from it. Larraine, get up here and show him how it's done."

He handed me his rifle. I aimed and took the shot. The coon tumbled, hitting branches in its descent and landed with a lifeless thud in the pine needles beneath the tree. Daddy and his friends roared with approval and slapped me on the back.

"Now bring the other one down."

I shot again and the second coon fell, landing a few feet from the first. More approval and slaps on the back.

"At's my girl. I told you she could shoot. Sure as hell outshot your drunk ass."

That was the way it went throughout the hunting season with Daddy and his friends. I was his Annie Oakley, the sharpshooter, and on exhibition. I was the girl who could drop two coons with two shots from a .22 caliber rifle.

By the end of fall, I had decided not to shoot anymore. This wasn't hunting for food. This was a sport for drunks who cut off the tails of the coons and left their bodies where they fell to bloat and rot. The coon tails were attached to the truck's radio antenna as trophies for all to see. There were a dozen or more of them that hunting season that went everywhere we went, trapped and waving in the wind on the antenna of Daddy's truck. If I had them today, I would not be able to point out to you the ones I killed, but I know I was responsible for at least a half dozen of those trophies.

I had dreams about the coons. The sound of the gunshot, then the animal tumbling, hitting branches over and over but never reaching the ground. Then, as if dreams could rewind, the scene was repeated again and again.

So one night I refused the rifle. It was a cold night, winter announcing its arrival with crisp winds, and the hounds were running. The wind distorted our hearing, making it hard to follow the path of the hounds. Daddy and his friends sat on the tailgate of his truck, drinking away the hour it took for the hounds to tree. We went into the woodland and followed their excited yelps. They sounded more urgent than on previous hunts. As we walked Daddy said that by the way the hounds were calling, it could be a bobcat or bear they were tracking. We reached the hounds, but there was no bobcat or bear, only three frightened coons high in the tree.

Daddy called back the hounds and dropped the first coon with one shot. One of his friends dropped the second with his third shot. Daddy held the rifle out to me.

"Last one's yours, Annie."

"Daddy, I don't want to shoot."

In an instant his feeling of pride and the attention he'd shown me the last four months were gone. It took less than five beats of the heart for the blue devils to return raging in Daddy's eyes.

"What the hell you talking about? Shoot that goddamn coon!"

He tried to push the rifle into my hands, but I refused to take it and told him again that I didn't want to shoot. He raised the rifle and pointed it down at me. He held it steady, his steel blue eyes squinting into the rifle sight. His eyes were the same color and shape as my own. I held his gaze, knowing that my eyes were now the only thing that made me human to him, and I hoped he would not take the shot.

Then as quickly as he raised and pointed the rifle at me, he whirled back to the tree, fired and brought down the third coon, but it wasn't a clean shot. The coon fell and landed at the base of the pine, twitching and moving its legs, running in place. Daddy took his pocket knife and cut off the tails of the first two coons and then the third as it still twitched.

He turned back to me. There was nothing in his face now but dark rage. "You think you're going to embarrass me in front of my friends? You ain't no better than a hound that don't do as it's told. You know what we do with hounds like that? We leave them in the woodland. You're going to stay right here 'til you hear the sound of my rifle, then you're going find your own way out of the woodland."

He called the hounds and leashed them, and he and his friends started the hike back through the woodland to the logging road and the truck. I watched as the last flicker of light from their carbide lamps faded, and I waited for the sound of the rifle. So this was my punishment for defying Daddy, to be left in the woodland like the hound that does not obey its master. I wasn't frightened. Daddy didn't know I had several things in my favor that would carry me out of the woodland. There was a full moon and Otha had taught me through games how to track.

"Larraine, ever living thing leaves a trail that ya can follow day or night. They leave their scent and the path they took. Close your eyes, Larraine, and see if ya can find me."

Otha and I had played this game many times inside the old farmhouse, in the yard and in the woodland. When I found him with my eyes still closed, Otha would jump out growling, pretending to be a bear. This always sent me into a fit of giggles. But tonight this wasn't a game, and Otha wouldn't be waiting for me.

The rifle shot came as the third coon stopped thrashing in the pine needles, no longer trying to run and hold onto life. I began to pick my way out. The scent of the hounds, carbide lamps, sweat and whiskey were faint now, but the small breeze coming from the direction they had taken was enough to follow. It was slow going. Now and again I found myself in deep brush or tangled in wild blackberry brambles that snagged my clothing and the skin underneath. When this happened, I knew I was off the path, going deeper into the woodland and I had to find my way back to an easier passage.

Before I emerged from the woodland, I could hear the men talking, and the faint light from the carbide lamps slowly grew. When I reached the truck I was unsure how much time had passed. They were sitting on the tailgate, still drinking. It took a moment for them to register that I was standing there. Daddy got up, grabbed me by the collar of my jacket, and tossed me into the bed of the truck.

"You ride home with the hounds tonight."

The blue devils took us at top speed back down the logging roads. The truck fishtailed into curves, throwing gravel that pelted down on me and the hounds. We choked on dust from the dirt road and slid from one side of the truck bed to the other, looking for anything to hold onto and brace ourselves.

In that moment I wanted more than anything for Daddy to put the rifle in my hand.

Jan Fink

Otha, Cordie, the farm and Velvet were now my only refuge. The magic they made of the simple things took away the pain and fear, giving me a brief window of what life and childhood should be. The neighbor boys always came on Saturdays, the races now a tradition. I didn't race but rode with them during the week. Every Wednesday they'd ride over and we'd leave early morning making trips to abandoned farms, taking our time, stopping under the shade of tall pines to eat leftover breakfast biscuits and chunks of hoop cheese. Our plan was to explore every old home place within riding distance.

It was the second week of that summer when I met Johnny. We were readying for a trip to the old Lunsford home place. Otha told us that last he heard the old barn was still standing, even full of plows, traces, bridles, and no telling what all; said if I found a curry comb to bring it home so we didn't have to share the one he used on his mules. The sun was up early and the heat with it. Cordie found an old canteen Otha used when he plowed, rinsed it out and filled it with cool water from the well. She was handing it to me when we heard the whinny. Our horses came to attention, looking down the lane, snorting and calling back a greeting. And there he was, riding a small paint pony.

Johnny approached us and dismounted, throwing his leg over the pony's head with flair like the Lone Ranger. He was towheaded with seashell ears, thin as a rail and small, a head shorter than me and two heads shorter than the boys. There was little tone to him, his face chalky white with deep-set eyes of a color I couldn't discern. He walked toward us, his head down, kicking the small stones along the path leading into the yard.

"Hey, y'all. I'm Johnny and I heard you got a riding club. I was thinking I might want to join your club. Well, that is if it don't cost nothing." His voice was so high-pitched it was almost girlish.

The boys laughed and punched at one another like boys do. James Lee, the oldest of our group, stepped up to Johnny, looking over his shoulder at the pony. "It don't cost nothing to ride with us, but you got to have a horse."

Johnny's face went red. "What you think I rode up here on?"

James Lee brushed past Johnny and circled the pony, looking it up and down. "Looking at this, I'd say half a horse."

The boys laughed again, and one spurred James Lee on, saying, "Half a horse for half a boy?"

Johnny's face grew redder; he swung his leg over his pony's back, took the reins and spit on the ground near James Lee's feet.

Cordie had heard enough and came down off the porch. "James Lee, me and Otha let all ya boys come over here anytime it pleases ya, but one thing we ain't gone let is a bully round here. Long as ya meeting up here on our place this boy got a right to ride with ya, same as anybody."

James Lee hung his head moving the dirt around with his boot where Johnny had spit. Then he turned to Cordie with a big smile on his face. "Ahh, Miss Cordie, we was just joshin. He can ride with us. Ain't no problem. I'll even share them good biscuits of yours with him." Johnny looked uncertain but fell in behind the boys with me and Velvet. I could hear James Lee muttering to the other boys soon as we were out of sight of Cordie.

I introduced myself to Johnny. "Cordie and Otha are my grandparents. I spend my weekends during school and the summers with them but wish it was all the time. I live in town about thirty miles from here. You just move here? Where you from?"

"I'm from everywhere and nowhere. My daddy moved us down here a few months back. I knew them was your grandparents. Daddy bought my horse from the Fields man that owns the grocery. He was the one told me about the riding club. Guess it was his way a saying welcome to the community. Fine welcome it was, the boys making fun of me and my horse."

"I think your paint is a fine horse. He's the first one I've ever seen, other than in books. Don't let James Lee bother you. He's got a bad mouth sometimes and acts tough. I don't pay him any attention. I enjoy riding along. We have races every Saturday and on Wednesdays we go exploring. We have a list of places to go this summer, mostly old home places. Cordie and Otha won't let me go far by myself so that's why I stick with the boys. But I do sneak off by myself once in a while and go to a favorite place of mine. Hope you'll come next Saturday for the races and keep riding with us. I think you'd like the place I want to add to the list. The ground there is covered with the devil's snuff." Johnny didn't answer but just kept his eyes on the back of James Lee's head.

It was an hour ride to the Lunsford home place. It was a vast expanse of flat land with a few trees and overgrown with high parched sagebrush that tickled the bellies of our horses as we rode deep into the fields. The barn was set back in the center of the land, made of lengths of rough-hewn timber. An uneven pile of fieldstone lay against the right front wall. The double doors were open, one with a rusted hinge that had given up, dropping the top section of the door at an odd angle. It looked like a broken wing.

James Lee shifted in his saddle, looking back at me and Johnny. "Hey, Johnny boy! You believe in ghosts? Barn doors are open! Maybe old man Lunsford is in there working on a piece a harness right now, and here we are interrupting him."

"I don't scare easy if that's what you're thinking, James Lee."

"Well, Johnny boy, we'll see. They're some things that'll scare anybody."

"Leave him alone, James Lee."

"Whoa! I think Larraine likes this half boy. What you going to do, tell Miss Cordie on me?"

"Just saying leave him be. Are we going to see what's inside? That's why we're here."

James Lee pulled four flashlights from his saddle bags and tossed one to me with that big smile back on his face. "You and Johnny boy can share. Oh, and Johnny boy, if I was you I'd be careful what I stuck my hand in cause there's no telling how many rattlers and copperheads holed up in this rickety old pile of timber."

It was a relief to get out of the sun. The barn was damp and dark, the only light filtering in from the broken-wing door. Otha was right; it was full of things to explore. Wooden boxes of all sizes lined the right wall, stacked five feet high. Above them hung mule collars, singletrees, traces, bridles and halters. At the rear was a wagon, its wood rotted away in some places and missing the front wheels. The left wall was littered with piles of dried corn cobs, feed buckets, broken chicken cages, small tools, hoe handles and troughs. We split up, me and Johnny looking through the wooden boxes while James Lee and the other boys sifted through the piles along the left wall.

Johnny was hesitant, opening the first box at a distance with an old fire poker he'd found on the barn floor. The first three boxes were empty. The next four were filled with rats' nests and droppings.

James Lee started clapping and yelled across the barn to me. "Larraine, look here at what I found!" He threw the curry comb a little too hard. It bounced off the wooden boxes between me and Johnny, almost hitting Johnny square in the face. I gave James Lee a hard look and didn't say thank you.

"You be sure and tell Otha and Cordie it was me that found it. Help me get back in good graces."

I ignored him and went back to looking through boxes. Johnny kept quiet, but the redness was back in his face. Anger was the only thing that put color in his pallid complexion.

Having found nothing of any value, we were down to only a few boxes when one paid off. Wrapped up in some old feed sacks was a pair of cowboy boots. They were black with soft gray uppers that were stitched in green leaf and red flower designs. Johnny and I were the only ones in the group that didn't have saddles or cowboy boots. I didn't mind riding bareback and actually preferred it. I liked the feel of Velvet's muscles moving beneath me.

The boots were dusty, the leather dull, but I hoped they'd fit me or Johnny. I handed them to him. "Here you try them on first."

He handed them back. "No, you go ahead. I think they're girl's boots. Sides, I plan to buy me a pair soon." I turned them upside down and shook a couple of granddaddy long-legs out before I pushed my feet into them. They were a little long in the toe, but I still had growing to do and was thrilled to have them.

When we got back, Otha was proud of the curry comb, rubbing it with a wire brush to take off the rust. I didn't give James Lee credit for finding it. Cordie helped me clean the boots inside and out, and then we rubbed them down with the oil Otha used on his mule collars and harness. When we finished they looked almost brand new.

That next Saturday I was surprised but glad to see Johnny and the paint coming down the lane, the last to arrive for the race. He joined the boys as they headed up the lane to line up at the starting place that we had marked with faded bandanas tied to cane poles.

Otha called out to them. "Hold up, boys. Larraine, ya a good rider now. Go get 'em cowboy boots. Ya and Velvet give it a try."

I joined the race and came in second to last, Johnny and his paint not far behind me. Two Saturday's later Johnny and I placed the same with the paint coming close to passing Velvet in the last race. Otha told me that Velvet was used as a racking horse and she had only one gait. To win a race, I'd have to break her gait and make her gallop.

I spent three weeks riding her up and down the lane, my heels nudging her sides, pushing her to run as fast as she could. She broke her gait the fourth week, her legs loose and running full gallop. I had to hold to her mane to stay on her back. Otha cheered from the front porch and ran out to meet me as I reined in Velvet.

"Ya ready to race now. Bet there ain't a one 'em boys' horses can beat Velvet!"

The day before the next race I took Velvet to the creek and washed her down with a bar of soap Cordie gave me. The next morning we were up at dawn, Cordie helping me braid Velvet's mane, tying off the braids with red ribbons. Otha dug up white clay and added a little water to it, and we put handprints on Velvet's chest to make her strong, circles around her eyes to make her see better, and lightning marks along her legs to make her run faster. Otha said Velvet was ready for battle, and the other horses would sense that. He was sure she would win.

And she did. Her long legs in full gallop carried us a length ahead of the geldings and stocky quarter horses the boys rode. Otha and Cordie were as proud and excited as I was. While Otha and I rubbed down Velvet, Cordie set up the ice cream freezer. The boys stayed the afternoon on the porch with us, taking turns cranking the freezer. They challenged me to more races in the future. I was ready anytime. I had never felt as free as when I was on Velvet's back, feeling her breathing, her muscles moving beneath me and the wind in my hair as we raced along. This day we had become not two but one.

FIVE

There were more races that summer, and Velvet and I won all of them. I was ready to expand my riding range and asked if I could make trips to Fields Grocery. Cordie thought it was a good idea. She took two feed sacks and tied them together with rope that I could drape across Velvet's back and bring home the things she needed from the store. Otha agreed, but since I'd be riding along the main road he made the first trip with me, telling me I must always ride on the side toward oncoming traffic. He walked beside me and Velvet and held the reins in case a passing car spooked her. Three cars passed us, and Velvet remained calm.

I made the trip to the store anytime Cordie needed flour, meal, honey or molasses. The boys told me that past the store there was a long dirt road that led down to the sulfur springs. Said the water smelled and tasted like rotten eggs, but it was a nice, peaceful place for riding. On my next trip to pick up supplies I went to the springs first. The ride down was difficult. The road was neglected, in disrepair, with deep furrows where heavy rains had washed away the soil and taken it downhill. Velvet went slowly, with guarded steps. The bottom of the road opened onto acres of land held within walls of tree-lined slopes reaching high, almost touching clouds. It was beautiful and eerily quiet, other than the trickling water of the springs.

Halfway into the open land Velvet stopped short. She held her head high, her ears at attention and her nostrils flaring, taking in a scent I could not detect. I urged her forward, but she refused, taking a few steps backward. The woodlands in Windham Springs were full of all kinds of wildlife. I thought she might have sensed a fox or possum. I dismounted, took the reins and led her toward the sound of the springs. She was still hesitant, looking from side to side, but followed. The woodlands were also full of rattlers and water moccasins, especially near water, so I watched the ground with each step.

We reached the springs and I waded in. Velvet stopped at the edge of the water and lowered her head to drink. Then she began to tremble, quickly backing away. I held to the reins and tried to comfort her, but suddenly she was wild. She pulled me backward with her, the bridle reins burning into my hands. I tied off the reins to a small oak, but this put her in full panic. I continued to talk to her, but she reared, trying to get free. The bridle snapped and she was off, running up the rutted road and out of the springs.

Velvet had pulled so hard on the bridle I was unable to untie the knot in the reins, so I had no choice but to leave them hanging on the oak and start the walk home. Two miles into the walk I could see Otha ahead running toward me. I knew I was in trouble and afraid something bad had happened to my Velvet. When Otha reached me, he wanted to know if I was okay and told me Velvet had come back to the farm without me and a bridle. He had feared the worst.

"Ya scared hell out of me and Cordie. I got the whole countryside out looking for ya! What happened? Velvet throw ya? Are ya hurt?"

I told him I'd gone to the springs, but Velvet hadn't thrown me. Something scared her, and the bridle was still there, tied to an oak.

"Ya should never go nowhere without telling us. Specially not to 'em springs. That place got bad things. Some of 'em ya can see, and some of 'em ya can't. Let's go get the bridle. I might can patch it. But ya got to promise me ya won't go down there no more by yourself."

When we got back to the farm, I checked on Velvet. Otha had left her in the barn lot to cool down. She was covered in sweat from the long run, still edgy and refusing to come near me. We sat on the front porch for hours that afternoon. Cordie and Otha wanted to know everything that happened at the springs. I told them about how scared Velvet had been as soon as we got to the clearing and then what happened at the edge of the water. Otha said it could have been a bobcat, and that was why Velvet still wouldn't come to me because she could smell it on me and my clothes.

Cordie disagreed.

"Back afore the Civil War, long afore that land came into your grandmother Ionia's family, the man that owned it brought in fifty slaves to build a hotel. People thought the water from the springs was a fountain of youth and could cure anything from rheumatism to toe itch. They had a dining hall, dancing, bowling and even a saloon 'til church folks complained and had it shut down. Sometimes there was as many as three to four hundred folks at the springs, some of 'em for a cure and others for the dancing and bowling.

Lot of folks round here still remember the stories about the springs. Most of 'em thought it was cursed and doomed from the start. During the war the Yankees came through Tuscaloosa to Northport, burning the bridge over the Warrior behind 'em. They worked their way up to Windham Springs and looted the hotel. It stayed open 'til May of 1917. It was a Sunday when a tornado twisted through and blew away everything. Somewhere up on one of them slopes there are big stones from the hotel porch. I've seen 'em.

They was a lot of people at the springs that Sunday, and a lot of 'em died in the storm. Velvet didn't sense or see a bobcat down at the edge of the water; she saw the ghost of someone the twister took. Story goes that there was a beautiful red-headed woman there that day. When the twister moved on and things got quiet, people went out searching for the missing. They found her at the spring, her head and shoulders under the water, her eyes open, her long red hair flowing with the current. Lot of people says they've seen her, and most times they never went back to the springs. That's what Velvet saw."

"Why could Velvet see her and I couldn't?"

"Sometimes when your mind is full, ya can't see all that's around ya. Animals can sense and see spirits long afore we do. I believe the dead come back cause I've seen my mama. They don't mean harm. They just want to be remembered. Lot of folks would laugh at me if I told 'em that. If ya love somebody and hold 'em in your heart, they come back. Sometimes ya can see 'em, and sometimes they just send ya a sign. I'm for sure Velvet saw that pretty red-headed lady today. Otha's right though. It's best ya don't go down there no more.

Jan Fink

When I returned home for the school year, I looked for Ionia, hoping I could see her like Velvet saw the red-haired lady in the springs. It was hard to know where to look. There was nothing left of Ionia in the house or yard. The house had been redecorated. The walls were white and the rooms filled with bland new furniture. Even the beautiful china that Toxie had laid out on the big table in the dining room for evening meals had been replaced with cheap imitation dinnerware that screamed up at you in bright white with fat blue ducks walking the rims of the plates. The yard had suffered the same treatment. Now treeless, it was flat and barren of anything but short-cropped grass, making it a grassland steppe covering any trace of landmarks holding childhood memories. I wanted to find the spot in that sea of green where Toxie and I had buried Old Mac beneath the hollyhocks but realized the bulldozer had probably taken him to the street along with Ionia's garden. I didn't see Ionia but knew if she chose to send me a sign, it would be in her garden. I could wait.

I stopped spending my afternoons in Ionia's house. I missed Toxie so much. I wanted her to be there in the kitchen so I could read to her and tell her about winning the summer races.

I missed Ionia reading my fortune and taking me away in bad times through teaching me to fly. Now there was only Grandfather Joe and his new wife spending their days in a house that was always overheated, the television always on and every room filled with smoke from Grandfather Joe's pipe.

At home things were also different. The blue devils were stronger, and they had been busy. The dog pen stood empty; the big television in the den was gone along with the radio in the kitchen. Daddy's prized collection of Hank Williams albums was no longer on the shelf in the living room. The saucer on the kitchen counter where he always left spare change, his wedding ring and the gold watch that Ionia gave him the last Christmas before she left us, was empty. Mama looked as if she hadn't slept all summer, her hair uncombed and matted. The house was in disarray, the furnishings moved to odd places, the curtains closed and the closets packed full of everything from jewelry and silverware to the kitchen toaster.

"Mama, is Daddy out hunting?"

"No. Don't know where he is."

"Then where are the hounds?"

"Gone, lost like the television, radio and all the other stuff."

"I don't understand."

"Your daddy has been throwing the dice and playing poker. He lost it all to a man that says he owes him more. The man's been calling, wanting his money. More money than we've got." Mama walked from window to window parting the curtains enough to look out.

"Listen to me, Larraine. Don't answer the phone or the door. When you leave for school in the mornings, go out the back door and cut through the yards. Don't use the street. You come home that same way. You hear me, Larraine?"

"Yes, Mama."

There were a lot of phone calls and knocks at the door from early morning 'til midnight. When Daddy wasn't at the fire station, he didn't come home 'til after midnight and left before the sun came up. Coming home from school one day, I forgot Mama's warning and used the street. As soon as I got to our house, a car pulled alongside me. The man in the passenger seat rolled down his window.

"Hey, girl! Your mama and daddy home?"

"I don't know."

"I don't see your daddy's truck, but that's your mama's car, ain't it?"

"Yes, but I don't know if she's home."

"You know where the keys to your mama's car are?"

I didn't answer this time. I turned away from him, walking down the side yard and then to the back door. Once inside I could still hear him yelling, "Hey, girl! Get back here! Where's the keys to your mama's car?" Mama was waiting in the kitchen in hysterics grabbing me by my sleeve.

"That was the man, wasn't it? What did you tell him?"

"Nothing."

"I saw you talking to him!" She tightened her grip on my sleeve, and for a moment I thought she was going to strike me.

"Mama, I told him nothing."

She let go of my arm and walked from window to window, peeking through the curtains, muttering, "Trying to kill me just like your daddy!

Mama never left the house. She had our groceries delivered. She kept vigil at the curtains and saw the man everywhere, even waking me at night to peer out the windows with her.

"Larraine! Come look! You see that little light from his cigarette? It's the man. The man is out there!"

"No, Mama. It's just a lightning bug."

"It's the man! See, the light from his cigarette is over there now!"

"A lightning bug, Mama. That's all. Go back to bed."

"I can't go back to bed. The man is out there pacing back and forth waiting for George to come home or one of us to leave the house! No safety! Nothing's safe! The man is going to take everything, including us!"

The man was always there, whether real or imagined, in Mama's mind.

Jan Fink

Little Brother rarely spent his summers on the farm now that he'd met friends his own age. He spent his time at their houses, staying overnight and playing in their backyards during the summer days. It was his safe place. Safety for me was getting out of there and back to the farm for the summer.

Otha had bought an old secondhand truck and came to pick me up. He named it Dawkins. There were holes in Dawkins' floorboard big enough to watch the pavement as we sped along. It had no windshield wipers, and we had to stop three times before we reached the farm to fill up on brake fluid. But Dawkins got us there. For the first week back I slept well and enjoyed the sun shining on my face through open windows and the quiet time we spent on the porch in the evening.

Race day came, but I didn't join in. The thrill and challenge were gone. I stayed on the porch with Cordie and Otha to watch. Johnny was late. I was afraid that with all the teasing James Lee put on him last summer, he'd decided not to come anymore. The race was just finishing when he came down the lane. He was still riding bareback but had bought himself a pair of red rubber cowboy boots like ones I'd seen in the five and dime. Johnny swung his leg over the paint's head, and the rubber boots made a squeaking sound when his feet hit the ground. James Lee stifled a laugh pretending to clear his throat.

"Y'all want a run another race? My paint got her legs now and she's faster than last summer."

James Lee looked to the other boys. None of them spoke, waiting for their leader to make the decision. "Not today, the horses are too hot. But we sure are looking forward to seeing you Wednesday, right boys?" The boys all smiled and nodded. We could hear them laughing before they were halfway down the lane.

Johnny lingered and joined me on the porch, sitting quietly 'til Otha and Cordie left to work the fields. He kept his head down, not making eye contact, his shrill voice quieter when he spoke this time. "Why didn't you race today?"

I shrugged. "Oh, I don't know. Guess I just got tired of it."

"Yeah, well, I wish they'd done another race today. Me and my paint would have won. I've been running her all winter. You know, like in training, and I tell you what. She's the fastest she's ever been. Sure as I sit here, we'd a won."

"Are you going to ride with us Wednesday? We're going to the place I told you about last summer, the one with the devil's snuff on the ground. The old Duck John home place, it's a pretty long ride but worth it."

"There ain't no such thing as devil snuff."

"Just wait and see for yourself. It's there because Otha told me old Duck John made a pact with the devil to have water all year round on his place."

"Still don't believe in no devil snuff, but I reckon I'll come along. See you Wednesday."

Johnny was first to arrive. His mama had packed him lunch and a Mason jar of sweet tea in an old worn-out school backpack. The weight of it pulled on his back, the straps taking turns sliding off his shoulders and down his arms. Cordie and Otha were already in the fields behind the farmhouse fighting a stand of Johnson grass so they could put in more crops. James Lee and the boys were late, so Johnny and I passed the time sharing the curry comb, brushing down Velvet and the paint.

It was mid-morning when they got there, James Lee riding out front. He stood up in his stirrups and motioned toward the porch. "Where's Miss Cordie and Otha?"

151

"Working a field. We'll pass them on the way out. The path in the woodland to the Duck John place starts about where they are."

"They know where we're going today?"

"No, didn't ask. They're busy."

"I know a better way of getting to Duck John's home place. We take the main road almost to Fields Grocery, then cut off on one of the old logging roads. It'll be wider than the path, and we won't have to ride single file. It'll cut some riding time too."

James Lee pulled his hat low on his forehead and took the lead. Johnny and I fell in behind the rest, riding side by side. No one spoke for the two miles it took to reach the small opening in the woodland along the main road. A half mile in the opening brought us to the logging road. It was weedy, and in some places knee-high pine saplings had sprouted trying to find the sun in the dense woodland. It was another half mile before James Lee spoke.

"Hey, Johnny boy, how come nobody told you that those new red rubber boots of yours clash with the colors of your pony? If I was that paint, I wouldn't have you on my back with them on."

"Shut up, James Lee. Leave me alone."

"Wish you wouldn't talk so loud. That voice of yours makes my ears want a turn inside out." The boys turned, looking back at Johnny and laughing. James Lee was stirring them up and loving it.

"Hey, boys, I think I got us a new name for Johnny boy. We gonna call him Johnny Red Boots!" The boys took his lead making their voices high, taunting and calling out, "Johnny Red Boots! Johnny Red Boots!"

"I said shut up! One day somebody's gonna shut that mouth of yours for you, James Lee. I ain't scared of you!"

"Johnny Red Boots, you better watch your own mouth. Remember what I told you last summer? There are some things that'll scare anybody."

I reined Velvet in, putting some distance between me and Johnny, us two, and James Lee and the boys. "You want to go back? We can go another day, just the two of us."

"I ain't going back. I ain't scared of James Lee or none of them."

It was an hour before we reached the Duck John place. Nothing was said for the rest of the ride, so I thought James Lee had had his fill of teasing for the day. The place was the same, the chimney still standing, the pond water clean and the devil's snuff even more abundant than the last time I'd been there. I told Johnny to step on one and it would release the snuff. He was amazed, stepping on one and then another, smiling as he watched the brown snuff explode into the air.

"I didn't think there was such a thing, but it shore looks like snuff. The devil's snuff. I just messed with the devil's snuff." That was all it took to get James Lee and the boys started.

"You call stepping on a few clumps messing with the devil's snuff, Johnny Red Boots? Let's show him messing with the devil, boys." James Lee and the boys jumped up and down on every piece of devil snuff, sending up a cloud of brown dust so thick it filled our noses and sent us choking and running. James Lee just stood there in the dust laughing.

"Now that, my boy, is messing with the devil. Johnny Red Boots, what you think the devil's gonna do about me messing with his snuff? Come up out of the ground and get me?"

"I hope he does, James Lee, and takes you back down to hell with him where you belong."

James Lee kept on laughing. Then he kicked up more devil snuff and mounted his horse. "Anybody want to go exploring with me?" The boys went along riding back down the logging road.

Johnny and I sat in the grass next to the pond throwing pebbles in, watching the water ripple. "Why you think they don't like me? I never done nothing to them."

"I don't know, maybe because you're somebody new to them."

"How'd you get started riding with them? They ain't mean to you."

"They all know Cordie and Otha and know if they were mean to me, Otha wouldn't have it and would put them on the road or worse."

"Well, they ain't gonna run me off, specially that James Lee. I don't need nobody to fight my battles. I do fine all by myself."

Johnny slipped his arms out of his backpack and put it on the grass between us. The zipper was broken, the opening held together by three big safety pins. He removed the safety pins, tucking them in the front right pocket of his jeans. He reached deep in the backpack and pulled out a Mason jar of tea, two sandwiches and a handful of fried potatoes wrapped in wax paper.

"You hungry? I got plenty." He handed me one of the sandwiches and set the fried potatoes and tea next to me.

155

"It's peanut butter and jelly. My mama made the peanut butter and the blackberry jelly too. She stirs the peanut butter up real good before she makes me a sandwich cause she knows I don't like too much oil."

We ate in silence, sharing the jar of tea and waiting for James Lee and the boys to return for the trip back to the farm. A half hour passed before we heard the sound of the horses coming down the logging road. James Lee and the boys tied their horses to the trees by the pond and approached Johnny.

"We found something real interesting right down the road a ways. Thought you might want to go back with us to check it out. I ain't never seen nothing like it. Maybe you can tell us what it is."

"I ain't interested in no more of your mouth or jokes. Just as soon stay right here."

"Ahh, Johnny, you still mad at us for teasing you about those red rubber boots and your little pony? We were just initiating you into our riding club. You ought to know you can't join any club without being initiated. All's well now and we're trying to include you. Like I said, I ain't never seen nothing like this in these woodlands. It's off the logging road. Come on and check it out with us."

"James Lee, he said he didn't want to go."

"I got ears, Larraine. I heard him. Well, Johnny, if you want to stay here with the little girl, go ahead. No skin off my back. Come on, boys, let's go back and give it another look."

"Wait up. I'll go with you." Johnny stood and started toward the paint.

"It ain't too far Johnny. We can walk. Larraine, you stay here and watch the horses for us. What we found ain't for the eyes of a squeamish girl."

I watched them walk away at a brisk pace. James Lee had his hand on Johnny's shoulder, conversation in low tones passing between Johnny, James Lee and the boys 'til they were out of sight. Then there was stillness and silence. I picked up more pebbles and tossed them into the pond. One by one they broke the surface of the water with a plop, then sent out silent ripples and the woodland quieted once again. I had been in a place like this before in the woodlands. That eerily quiet day when Velvet saw the red-haired lady at sulfur springs. The thought frightened me, so I busied myself by putting the picnic leftovers in Johnny's backpack. But as soon as I touched the backpack my fear increased.

At that moment I knew something bad had entered the woodland. The bad had crept into the woodland, threatening like the silent flicker of a snake's tongue before the strike. I thought of the red-haired lady and how she must have run when the sound of the tornado roared into the springs. Like her, I wanted to run, but fear held me on the bank of the pond, the devil's snuff still strong in my nostrils. Fear kept me there 'til the horses began screaming. They pulled at their tethered bridles, reared and kicked at one another in their attempt to break free.

There was another voice mixed in with their panicked neighs. It was Johnny's voice, shrill and piercing, screaming words I could not understand. I ran toward the sound of his voice, clumsy and tripping, all of it playing out in a sluggish, dreamlike state. His screams were close, just off the logging road somewhere in the woodland. I ran faster coming to a small clearing and saw James Lee raising a broken pine limb and slamming it down on Johnny as the others kicked at him.

Johnny lay in the pine needles, twitching like the wild-eyed coon that Daddy didn't give grace to kill with a clean shot. His eyes were open, but the last blow of the limb from James Lee silenced his screams. His head was swollen, covered in rusty blood, giving off a metallic smell that mixed with the scent of pines. There were cuts and bruises on his face and down his arms creating colors that should not be on someone's skin. I was frozen, not knowing why this was happening or what to do, only knowing that I could hardly bear to look at Johnny.

James Lee raised the limb again.

"No, James Lee!"

He looked up, dropped the limb and raced to me, grabbing me by my shoulders and shaking me.

"What the hell are you doing out here? I told you to wait with the horses!"

"Why are you doing this to Johnny? Tell the boys to stop! You're killing him!"

"Shut up, you stupid little bitch! You should have done what I told you and stayed with the horses!"

The boys continued to kick Johnny, his body tossed from one boot to the other like a boneless rag doll. James Lee let go of my shoulders and sank his fingers deep into my arm to pull me out to the logging road, back to Duck John's place and the waiting horses. He pushed me down hard into the devil's snuff and then picked up Johnny's backpack.

"You stay right here. You better not move from this spot 'til I get back. You hear me?" I nodded yes; fear had taken my voice. I watched, afraid to move or speak as he ran back down the logging road with the backpack. Time slowed, and it seemed like forever 'til he came back.

He didn't look at me, just walked circles around me, his head down, face red, kicking up the devil snuff with his bloody boots. Then he walked over to a pine near the pond and leaned against it, spitting on the ground.

"Now what am I supposed to do with you, Larraine?"

I remained still and silent, but the voice in my head was screaming. *Tuck it away! Tuck it all away!*

"Yep. That's the question. What do I do with you? Any ideas, Larraine?"

"Find the boxes. Open the boxes. Tuck it away. Tuck it away."

"What'd you say?" James Lee looked out toward the pond. "What boxes? Ain't no boxes out here, Larraine. Just me and you."

He walked back to me. I could feel him standing over me, looking down, but I couldn't look up. I focused on his boots.

The blood peppered with the devil's snuff that covered them was beginning to dry and smelled of rust and earth.

"You really liked that useless little queer, didn't you?"

I kept still, my head down, afraid to move or answer. James Lee laughed and stamped his foot.

"Well, Larraine, fess up. You liked him, didn't you? Do you even know what a queer is?" He stamped his foot again and slapped the top of my head.

"I don't know what you're talking about. Why are you doing this, James Lee?"

"I'm doing this for you, Larraine. Because he *was* a queer. Running around in them red rubber boots. Too bad you liked him cause he would of never been boyfriend material. Larraine, here's your lesson of the day. A queer don't like girls. They fuck each other in the ass. That's what they like. Johnny Red Boots had a bad mouth on him too. Never knew when he needed to keep it shut. Look at Johnny boy now. I shut his goddamn mouth, but before I shut his mouth, I fucked the little queer. Yeah, I give him what he wanted. I shoved that limb right up his ass. We put some good old backwoods country justice on him. This ought to be a lesson to you too, Larraine. People ought to know when to keep their mouths shut. You getting my message? Look at me and tell me you're getting my message."

I hesitated and he kicked my thigh, leaving a print of blood and devil snuff on my jeans. I raised my head and nodded yes. He went to Velvet, untied her and stood holding her reins.

"Get on your horse." I did as he said and reached down for the reins but James Lee kept holding them looking down at the ground. When he did look up he was calm and smiling, flecks of blood dotted his face, his hair and the brim of his hat.

"Best you go on home now. We're just playing with him, no harm done. We'll clean him up and get him on his way in no time. But if anybody asks, the last time you saw Johnny Red Boots, he was headed home on that little paint of his."

I didn't answer. I was trembling so hard I couldn't find my voice. I reached for the reins again, but James Lee still wouldn't give them up. And now the smile had left his face.

"Now tell me, Larraine. When was the last time you saw Johnny Red Boots?"

All I could manage was to nod my head.

"I wanna hear you say it, Larraine!"

"Going. Going home on the paint."

"Good girl! We'll see you Saturday for the races."

James Lee handed me the reins, his smile back, then he slapped Velvet's hindquarters hard, causing her to bolt and race down the logging road.

Cordie and Otha were still in the fields. It gave me time to calm down, trying to stop the trembling. I went to bed early, eating no supper, telling Cordie I wasn't feeling well. I was afraid to go to sleep and even more afraid to wake up. I was on the porch when Johnny's daddy got to the farm early the next morning. He introduced himself to Cordie and Otha and told them his boy Johnny hadn't come home from the ride yesterday. Said the paint was found this morning just down the main road near Fields Grocery. She was all scraped up and bloody like she'd been running through briars in the woodland. He was afraid the paint had thrown Johnny and wanted Otha to help look for his son in the woodland near where the horse was found.

"Shore, I'll help ya. Larraine, did Johnny ride with ya and the boys yesterday?"

"Yes, sir."

"Where'd ya go?"

"Down the logging road to the Duck John Place."

"Ya ride home with him?"

"No, sir. Johnny left for home early." Otha looked at me with trusting eyes. At that moment I knew that if lying was a sin, I had committed my first sin.

"I know 'em old logging roads," Otha told Johnny's daddy. "The paint might a run up on a rattler, got spooked, and took off running taking Johnny out through 'em thick bushes and trees."

Otha left with Johnny's daddy and a handful of other men, and I sat on the porch hour after hour waiting. It was dark before Otha returned. He looked tired when he climbed the porch steps and called Cordie out of the house.

"We found the boy. Been laying out there in the woodland all night. We carried him out to the main road, and his daddy loaded him in his truck and headed to town and the hospital. Looked like the boy took some hard bumps and a bad fall when the paint bolted. From the looks of it, I don't think that boy will ever have his legs again or any sense. That's what I been telling ya, Larraine, about taking off riding on ya own. It just ain't safe riding in the woodland alone."

I wanted to tell Otha the truth about everything. That I had lied. But he didn't have to worry. I'd never ride in the woodland again. I wanted to tell him that the devil was still there at the Duck John Place. And that the devil had made another pact in the woodland with James Lee and the boys. And maybe with me through my silence and lies. And that never again would I feel safe.

I wanted to tell him that something in me died in the woodland. But the fear that put the lies on my tongue kept me still and silent. I tucked it all away in one of the dark boxes inside my head.

Jan Fink

EIGHT

It had been five years since I refused to take the rifle that fall night in the woodland. As Daddy stood pointing the rifle down at me, he'd seen something in my eyes. Something that told him I was no longer afraid of him. He also knew that if I'd taken the rifle that night, I would have shot, but not to bring down the wild-eyed coon. What he saw in my eyes that night made him cautious. He stopped our weekly target practice. We had no more hunting trips; he took all his guns from the house and hid them.

The madness at home escalated. Mama was sure that she would not survive the nightly beatings at Daddy's hand. She began calling the police after the first hit. It was laughable. A small town takes care of its own. The fire station was in the same building as the police department. They were all good friends. When the officers responded, it was always the same. They'd say to Mama, "Now Ruby, you and these kids go on back to bed. Just let George sleep it off. All will be fine come morning."

No sooner were they out of sight than the beating began again.

Little Brother and I slept in our clothes, ready to run. Mama would wait up each night, listening for the sound of Daddy's truck pulling into the driveway. She'd wake us, and we'd flee out the back door and into her car. We'd spend the night driving up Highway 69 into the countryside, then thirty miles out we'd cross over to Highway 43 and drive back to town. If Daddy's truck was still in the driveway, we'd make the loop again and again 'til dawn, when he was back at work. I learned to drive, making the loop from town to countryside, countryside to town with Mama in the backseat sleeping and Little Brother up front with me, his head on my lap mile after mile.

We were always running, never safe. One night Mama woke us at the first sound of the truck. The three of us scrambled into our shoes and out the back door. Daddy was waiting for us, standing in front of Mama's car, holding a cinder block. The drink had made his mouth slack, his eyes vacant, unreadable. He lifted the cinder block above his head.

"Stupid sumbitchs! Do you think I don't know what you're doing? I've been watching you get in that car from the window every night. I know what you're doing. Get in the car! Go ahead! Get in the goddamn car! Take a ride."

We stood silent, unsure. Mama took our hands, and we walked slowly toward the car. Daddy gave us a thin-lipped smile and started to sing.

There are those who'd like to change the way I'm livin'.
It seems they just don't like the way I am.
Tomorrow I may live the way they're thinkin',
Oh, but tonight I just don't give a damn.

He laughed, lowered the cinder block, and cradled it in his arms rocking it back and forth. We reached the car door. Daddy raised the cinder block above his head, laughed louder and shouted.

"Go for it! Go for it, bitch!"

Mama let go our hands and reached for the door handle. The windshield suddenly caved inward, the cinder block wedged into the glass. Daddy pulled it free and slammed it down once more. This time the windshield exploded sending little cubes of glass inside the car. The cinder block rested on the driver's seat. All we could do was run back inside.

I was never safe after that, running in every waking hour. Soon I ran in my sleep. The first of the recurring nightmares came after the night when we knew Daddy would always be waiting by the car. We'd lost our rescue loop. The nightmare was always the same: The cinder block. The windshield. Then

I'm running, running. Chased by something bigger than me, its breath hot on the back of my neck. It has the dank smell of an animal I don't recognize. I dare not look back in fear of being caught. It chases me through the house. Into the yard. Up Highway 69 and down Highway 43 making the loop back to the house. Over and over again 'til I awake. Exhausted. Covered with sweat.

Night after night I ran, chased by an animal I had no control over. Even in my waking hours I was exhausted, the nightmare still in my head. My brain wouldn't let go of it.

The last nightmare began the same as every night for the past two months, but this time there was a difference.

I am running as fast as I can, but my legs are thick, gnarled and twisted. When I try to run on my crooked legs I stumble, go down on one knee and struggle to get back on my feet. By the time I'm up and running again, it's too late. The animal smell is stronger now, its breath too close. And now its hand, coarse and rough, is on my shoulder, gripping hard, pulling me back to face it.

I turn and look back into the eyes of something I have only seen in books. The gorilla begins to laugh, reaches for the top of its head and grabs a crest of fur and pulls. The head comes off in its hand, a flattened mask that it holds out for me to see. But it still has a head where the mask was, the head of my daddy. Its laughs are loud and piercing, each laugh becoming sharper, more grating and ear-splitting. The coarse gorilla hand is still on my shoulder, holding me in place, shaking me violently. Its other hand holds the mask out, pushing it closer and closer to my face. I open my mouth to scream, but no sound comes from me. Someone is screaming, but the screams are not mine.

I woke trying to run. My legs were normal, flailing beneath the bed covers, my eyes open. I was no longer asleep, but I still heard the screams.

"He's killing me! Jesus, help, he's killing me!"

I stumbled from bed, my legs weak from nightmare running. The screams were coming from the kitchen. I reached the door and found Mama on the floor. Daddy was on his knees straddling her, delivering blow after blow to her face and chest. A paring knife lay next to his right knee. Daddy's T-shirt was ripped, bloody and hanging off his left shoulder.

I understood, Mama had fought back. The Early American kitchen table was on its side against the wall, two of its matching chairs sprawled in the middle of the floor. The smell of blood and fear came back. That same fear that had crept quietly into me and the woodland the day Johnny's legs and mind were taken. I stood and watched as Daddy struck Mama over and over. Now no cries were coming from her.

I waited for the voice in my head. To hear those words. "Tuck it away. Tuck it all away." But this time the voice didn't come. The dark boxes were full.

It was then that I knew I could hold no more fear. I picked up one of the chairs. It was solid and heavy and easy to hold as a baseball bat. I raised the chair over my right shoulder. Like playing ball in school I was up to the plate. I assumed the stance.

"Batter up."

I swung, striking Daddy's right shoulder. He fell to the left but he was still punching Mama's chest.

"Ground ball."

I assumed the stance again and swung harder this time. I make contact with the same shoulder. He slid across the linoleum floor into the stove.

"Fly ball."

He got to his feet and started toward me, his eyes dark and furious. I held the stance, let him get close, and then swung again. The third hit sent him slamming into the refrigerator. Up to the plate again, I swung over and over. He sank to the floor and held up his arms to deflect the blows, but I kept swinging.

"Home run! Home run! Who's the sumbitch now, Daddy? Who's the sumbitch?"

I heard the bones in his arms cracking, but I couldn't stop swinging. He began to moan, making crying sounds.

He fell to his side, still holding his arms above his head, waiting for the next swing, but I was finished. I was through with fear. I had graduated to violence.

The world was a sinister, lifeless, uncertain and unrelenting place. I was guarded and ill at ease about everything. I felt mindless. Numb. The only way I knew my heart still beat was by counting. Seventy-two beats a minute, four thousand three hundred twenty beats an hour. And when I reached one hundred and three thousand six hundred eighty beats, a day had passed. Then I'd start all over counting, marking off the days by the beat of my heart.

Even the magic that Cordie and Otha tossed into my childhood mind through their lessons and stories waned. I didn't ride Velvet anymore. Her magic had left me too. I walked the pastures with the cattle, plodding along beside them as they grazed. There was no paternal or maternal in my life. I was cattle that was fed and nothing more, my insides empty, dying a little more each day.

Otha once told me all animals needed salt to live. I followed the cattle and took my place among them, standing in the sun, licking the salt block.

NINE

Daddy was in a cast for six weeks. I'd broken four of his fingers and his right arm. After that night in the kitchen he stopped drinking. The house was quiet, Mama's late night screams and beatings ceased. Daddy took an interest in the kind of new music I listened to on the radio. He brought home Beatles, Bob Dylan and James Brown albums and allowed me to play them on his oak console stereo.

I wanted to believe I had stopped the blue devils. That I had done what Jesus had failed to do. It was only 'til the cast came off that Daddy made direct eye contact with me and I knew that I had stopped nothing. Within another week the blue devils were back. Their voices raged from Daddy's mouth, their fists became his, their gait, stance and all-consuming anger filled him. Daddy became nothing more than their host.

As the blue devils raged at home the outside world also raged. In 1963, as I sat in class, the intercom announced the assassination of President John F. Kennedy. My classmates cheered, drew Confederate flags on notebook paper and ran through the halls waving their paper flags and shouting, "The South will rise again!" I watched them joyously celebrate the death of our president who supported Civil Rights and had promised to end segregation. I thought of Toxie and her stories about slavery and segregation and what living in the South had always held for her. That day I was ashamed to be a southerner.

I made very few friends in school and did not date. I could not bring them to my home to be witness to our secret existence. I also could not bring myself to fight Daddy anymore for fear of becoming the very thing I'd thought of from an early age. Becoming a natural born killer. To end him and the blue devils.

In October 1965 Grandfather Joe passed away with little to no fanfare. He was buried alongside Ionia in a small country cemetery two miles west of Windham Springs. His name was chiseled into the large headstone marking the three cemetery plots that Ionia had purchased years before her passing. She wanted it to be the last resting place, side by side for her, Joe and her youngest son, George. Daddy stood at the gravesite with a bottle of Wild Turkey cursing them both, saying he'd never be put by their side. He disappeared for two days then came home still drinking, angry, smelling like sour earth and threatening everyone, "If you put me in the ground next to them I'll come back and get every one of you and take you back to hell with me!" It was a week before he stopped the threats.

My first year in high school I took a part-time job at a chicken restaurant, working after school and during summer vacations. It paid fifty cents an hour and I saved every penny. It was my plan to freedom. With my tiny income Mama had grand dreams for me. She wanted me to become an opera singer and now lamented that she didn't take Ionia up on voice and music lessons. I had nothing near a singing voice so Mama decided it best that I save my money for a nose job and a chance at becoming a model or even a movie star. She pulled out all her movie magazines and studied the star's photos, picking out new hairstyles and the new nose I'd buy with my savings. She enrolled me in the Sylvia Pitman School of Modeling where hours were spent walking with books balanced on my head, learning how to put on makeup, style my hair and walk a runway. Within three months at the modeling school it was obvious that no matter how much training they gave me they couldn't take away my tomboy ways or make me graceful. Mama soon lost interest, but it was just as well. I had my own dream. It wasn't to be a singer or get a nose job, model or become a star. I saved my money and dreamt of freedom.

In March 1967 the late John F. Kennedy's hope to end segregation became a reality. A federal district court ordered the Alabama state board of education to integrate all public schools by the next fall. There were two students bused from their area schools to my high school. Belinda was in my English class. She was quiet and edgy and sometimes fearful, with good reason. Jacob was in my art class. He was extremely talented and un-phased by the constant taunting. The same classmates from earlier years that celebrated the death of Kennedy made Belinda and Jacob's school year one of misery. They bumped into them, knocking their books from their hands. They refused to sit next to them in class and called out in the halls, "Nigger coming!" When I picked Belinda or Jacob as a class project partner I received the same. I was called "The Nigger Lover." There were threats also. Threats that were never reprimanded by any of the teachers. They turned a blind eye and deaf ear to it all. There was, and still remains, an attitude of unkind injustice in the South.

I continued working after school and during summers, but my weekends were still spent on the farm. I loved the time, sitting on the porch listening to Otha's stories and watching Cordie, like a silver swan pointing and guiding us through the day.

The year of my high school graduation Otha asked if he might sell Velvet. He and Cordie had struggled and never completely recovered their losses since the summer of the tornado years before. They needed money and one less animal to feed and care for.

Otha had never asked me why I no longer rode Velvet. I think he assumed I had outgrown my love for her. I was grateful that he didn't ask. I had not ridden Velvet since the trip with Johnny to Duck John's place. James Lee and the boys came to the farm every weekend for a year after that day. Sometimes James Lee came alone. He would sit across from me, his boots propped up on the wood cookstove, make small talk with Otha and Cordie, never taking his eyes off of me. I knew he came to make sure I had remained quiet. After a year he and the boys seemed satisfied and never came again. I agreed to let Velvet go but still couldn't tell Otha why I no longer had the desire to ride among the trees. And that not only did the blue devils live in my home but a devil lived in the woodland also.

I spent my last day with Velvet and watched as they loaded her in the trailer for the trip to her new home. She was one of the good pieces of my childhood, one of the best. I wanted to go back and have those days with her once more but childhood had ended that day in the woodland. At the moment I heard Johnny's screams and looked down at him lying in the pine needles I knew the world was not right. I knew that my childhood would be left in the woodland, but the memory of that day that I tucked away in the dark boxes in my head would remain forever.

After graduation I worked longer hours, hid my weekly salary and watched as the blue devils grew stronger. Coming home from work I'd often find Daddy passed out on the front porch or in his truck slumped over the steering wheel, music from his eight-track tapes blaring in the night. Those were the good nights. On the bad nights Mama would attempt to lock him out of the house. Daddy circled the house and broke out windows with the butt of his rifle as we locked ourselves in our bedrooms, hoping that his rage would burn out before he battered down the bedroom doors.

Mama's frequent headaches became constant, often sending her to bed for days. Nothing seemed to help but morphine, and the doctors gave it to her often, without thought of the consequences. Morphine became Mama's blue devils. A shot a day became two a day, then more. Morphine ravaged her body, took away her beauty and aged her into a pale, corpse-looking pin cushion that stared up with colorless eyes from dingy sheets. It was only when she was near death that the doctors stopped the injections and sent her to re-hab. She was never the same again.

TEN

Cordie and Otha weren't aware that Mama was in such a condition. I hitched rides with relatives for my weekend visits to the farm. They often asked about Ruby and I told them she was fine; she'd just been under the weather lately. I wanted to spare them the truth. Cordie and Otha were older and struggling for their own survival. They continued to work the fields during the day growing vegetables for their table but they were no longer able to work a cash, cotton crop. Otha took a night job as a watchman at a local dump. The job provided a little income and he was allowed to bring home discarded items that he cleaned and repaired. Cordie called them treasures and proudly showed me her water kettle, chest of drawers and straight back chairs that Otha had cleaned and re-worked for her. There was such a contentment and gratefulness about the smallest things that life offered up to them.

It was late summer, the crops offering up the last of its bounty that we sat on the porch, Cordie shelling peas and me waiting for Otha to tell a story. It had always been our nightly routine during long hot summer weekends. He could take the slightest event in his day and expand it into a glorious tale where he was more often than not the hero of the tale. I loved his stories, but that night he sat silent, patting his foot on the porch floor, looking out at the lane. He cleared his throat and turned to me.

"Larraine, ya remember that scrawny boy with the paint pony that used to ride with ya and the boys?"

My mind locked. Even the summer heat couldn't stop the rush of chills that set me to trembling. I didn't want to hear what Otha had to say, but knew in my heart what was coming. I sat silent, looking down at the porch floor, avoiding eye contact with Otha.

"I know ya remember him, Larraine. Ya was right here on this porch the morning his daddy come looking for him. His name was Johnny."

"Yes sir, I remember Johnny."

"Well, over the years ya ain't brought him up or ask about him. Since the paint throwed him in the woodland he been in a wheel chair all this time. Just like I said the day we found the boy after the accident, he didn't never have his legs again or any sense. Cordie and some other women from the church been taking turns going over and cooking and cleaning and helping the boy's mama anyway they could. His mama told Cordie the boy never spoke another word after he was brought out of 'em woods."

Otha turned from me and looked back at the lane. I knew I should say something. Anything. I clenched my teeth to stop them chattering and spoke through them.

"How is he?"

Cordie answered. "The Lord took him last Monday. The boy weren't nothing but skin and bones, a empty shell. It was a blessing in a way that the Lord took him home and out of his misery. I don't think I ever seen a mama take it so hard. Johnny was her only child, ya know?"

That old familiar fear came back taking me to the woodland and the sound of the limb striking and the screams. The fear started like a snake winding itself tightly around and up my spine, the snake's head poised and ready to strike the back of my neck. Otha looked back at me, waiting for a response, but I knew that if I moved or spoke the snake would strike.

"Johnny's daddy come over Monday evening to tell us about the boy passing. He thanked me for helping find his boy in the woodland that day and Cordie for all she done for Johnny's mama. They put him in the ground Wednesday. His daddy sold the paint pony to pay for the burying of his boy. When we men went to fill in Johnny's grave his mama fell right down on that pile of dirt, refusing to let us cover her boy. It took me and Johnny's daddy both to pick her up and carry her out of the cemetery afore we could bury Johnny. Me and Cordie thought ya would like to know. Ya all right, Larraine?"

I waited. Then spoke. The snake that was wrapped tightly around my spine didn't strike.

"I'm sorry. I'm sorry about Johnny."

"Well, one more thing, Larraine. That James Lee was at the funeral and acting all tore up about Johnny dying. All the time I have knowed James Lee I always took him with a grain a salt. He got that cocky attitude, ya know. A attitude he ain't never out-growed. Can't really say I trust him no further than I could pick him up and throw him. He was acting a little too tore up and I didn't see him shed one tear when us men went to fill in the grave. Matter a fact, he picked up a shovel and joined in, shoveling dirt real fast down on Johnny's casket and he was smiling the whole time. I know James Lee picked on Johnny right from the start when he went to riding with y'all. If something else happened in the woodland that day other than the paint getting spooked and throwing Johnny, ya would tell me, right, Larraine?"

Fear took my tongue. Then for the second time I looked into Otha's eyes and sinned. I lied.

"Nothing, Otha. Nothing else happened."

"Afore ya got here Friday James Lee come by and he says he's coming over tomorrow to check on ya. See how ya taking Johnny's passing. He says since ya don't have Velvet no more he gone bring along one of his other horses so y'all can go riding and talk about things."

The snake struck, sinking its fangs deep into the back of my neck. Searing hot pain raced to the top of my head. I could taste the poison along with the lies on my tongue. My vision blurred and for a brief moment there were no sounds in the world. I knew what things James Lee wanted to talk about. I also knew James Lee would if he could end me. I was the weak link to his transgression. I was a door he needed to close. The snake withdrew its fangs then struck again filling my head with more poison, sending me to the porch floor.

I woke early the next morning. Cordie was there at my bedside waving a paper fan and holding wet cloths to my forehead to cool me.

"How ya feeling? Me and Otha been worried about ya. Ya always been tough, never knowed ya to fall out like that. Was it us telling ya about Johnny that got ya so upset? If so, we sure are sorry. Didn't know ya was that close to the boy."

"No, Cordie. It wasn't anything you said. It was the heat, I guess. The heat and a bad headache. That's all it was." Cordie smiled down at me and waved the paper fan faster. I had become so efficient in the art of lies.

"James Lee is already here, out on the porch talking to Otha. He brought along another horse for you like he said he was gone do. It's still early and cool out. Not near as hot as yesterday. Ya always loved horses and riding. It might make ya feel better to get out for a while. Ya want me to tell James Lee ya be out in a minute?"

"No! Tell him no. Tell him I don't feel well or want to ride with him today. You'll tell him that for me, will you, Cordie?"

I could hear Cordie on the porch speaking in low tones. Then, James Lee expressing his concern for me not feeling well and promising to return the next weekend to check on me. I waited 'til I knew he had left the porch and was far from the farm. I walked to the main road and caught a ride to town and home.

I spent the rest of the day going through my closet picking out only what I could carry in a backpack. The tightness in my spine, the throbbing searing pain in my head and the taste on my tongue of poison and lies came and went with only one thought in between. Run! Run! Run! The next day I reported to work and spoke with my manager, Elaine, gave my notice and asked her for the names of small towns north of us.

"How far you wanting to go?"

"I've been saving pretty much all my salary since I started working here. I've got a little over six hundred dollars. How far would that take me?"

She laughed, pulled off her apron and picked up an order pad and pencil from the counter. She scribbled the name "Saint Florian" in big letters across the pad and handed it to me, then opened the register, pulled out three twenties and placed them in my hand.

"I ain't gonna ask you why you're running. That way anybody coming around here asking questions, well, I don't know nothing. That sixty I just give you is a tip and I'll write you a check for the hours you put in last week. You've been a good worker. I hate to see you go. But I understand. You ain't the first I've seen over the years that had to up and run. How quick you leaving?"

"As soon as I finish my shift."

"Saint Florian is a little town in Lauderdale County, almost to the Tennessee line. The money you've got will get you there with plenty left over to get a new start. It ain't much of a town but its rich in German heritage. They have a lot of festivals that you could maybe work in the booths to make a little money. Hand me that pad, I've got a friend that runs a little deli sandwich shop up there. She has a booth at all the festivals and might even be able to use you full time at her deli. I'm gonna add her name and the address of her deli. I want you to look her up as soon as you get there. Name is Sue Satterfield. You go first thing and talk to her. I'll call her and vouch for you as to being a good worker.

Sue's got a real mouth on her. She don't take no crap from no one and expects her workers to be workers. She tells it like it is, but don't let that upset you. She's a good woman and will help you anyway she can. I'm assuming you're going by Greyhound?"

ELEVEN

Elaine drove me to the bus station after my shift, and I boarded at dusk for my first bus ride. I'd never been more than thirty miles from home. The three hour trip seemed much longer with stops in every little small town along the way. In each town there was a rhythm of un-boarding and re-boarding, the voices and faces of passengers constantly changing. Through half the ride a talkative young man sat next to me, telling me his life history. He was going farther than Saint Florian, all the way to Tennessee where he'd be working as a logger. He'd broken up with his high school sweetheart and wanted to get as far out of Alabama as he could. On one stop he bought me a Coca Cola from one of the big red machines out front of the bus depot. Then we re-boarded, traveling through farmland. He watched out the window pointing out white-washed farmhouses, fields of corn and grazing cows.

"I hope I'm not bothering you. I talk a lot when I'm nervous." He smiled and looked out the window again.

"No, you're not bothering me. Why are you nervous?"

"I've never been out of Alabama. When I boarded in Mobile I was excited about the job and leaving Alabama but now Tennessee seems like a really far-a-way place. Guess that's why I'm nervous. How about you? You ever been out of Alabama?"

"No. I've never been far from home."

He fell silent, looking back out the window. Then suddenly he grabbed my hand and shouted.

"Look! Horses! Must be two dozen or more!"

The horses stood along the fence line of the pasture, heads raised and watching us pass. There were white and chestnut mares, bays, solid blacks, small Shetlands and there among them were three paint ponies. The reality of leaving rushed me and with it came tears. And with it also came the fear that there might not be any place far enough away to flee to and leave the past behind. I turned away from the young man and we did not speak again 'til I got off in Saint Florian and he smiled and wished me good luck.

I stayed in the depot pretending to be waiting to board another bus, dozing now and then 'til late in the morning. There was a grocery store directly across the street. I bought a soda, an apple and a pack of crackers for breakfast. At the checkout I asked for directions to Sue Satterfield's deli. It was less than three blocks away.

The deli was not much more than a hole in the wall, no tables or chairs just a long counter with stools banked on the other side with deep trays filled with bread, meats, cheeses, dressings and vegetables. Six people were in line at the counter so I waited 'til they got their sandwich orders and left. The young man behind the counter was incredibly thin, long-limbed with freckled skin, blue eyes and crinkly crimson hair. He stood waiting for my order and I stood there trying to find my voice. I had rehearsed what I planned to say while passing the night at the bus depot but now couldn't remember a word of it.

The young man cleared his throat. "Can I help you, ma'am?"

I blurted out. "Sue Satterfield."

He left the counter, walked to the double doors along the back wall, pushed the right door open a crack and yelled, "Mama! Someone here to see you!"

The sound of clanging pots and a mixer running wafted through the crack in the door, then a raspy, intimidating voice shouted out, "Give me a damn minute, will you? Got my hands full right now!"

Ten minutes passed before the sound of the mixer quieted and Sue Satterfield burst through the double doors wiping her hands on her apron and looking annoyed. The young man pointed to me. Sue looked in my direction, hands on her hips, shifting her weight from one foot to the other. She was half the size of her son, low and stocky but with the same freckled skin and hair even more crinkly and fire-engine red than his. She wore it back-combed and upswept into a tight bun high on the top of her head. Moments passed, Sue staring in my direction, waiting impatiently for me to speak.

"Miss Satterfield, my manager Elaine at the restaurant where I used to work told me to get in touch with you when I got to town."

"She did, did she?"

"Yes, ma'am."

"You got a name, girl?"

"Sorry, ma'am. Yes, I'm Larraine."

"Well, now, we're getting somewhere. Elaine called me right after she put you on the Greyhound. I swear to God, that woman thinks I'm the Mother Teresa of Saint Florian! So what might you be? Are you homeless, a runner, pregnant, a thief, on drugs or a lost soul?"

"I guess a runner and a lost soul."

"Running got you here. You look strong enough to do the work. With the festivals coming up I need the help and that'll help you. As to being a lost soul, ain't much I can help you with in that department. Can't nobody find your soul, but you. The way I operate is simple. If you do right by me, I'll do right by you. You do wrong by me?" Sue paused and cleared her throat. "I'm for everything that's good and against everything that's bad. You don't want to be bad to Sue Satterfield."

"Yes, ma'am."

"By yes ma'am does that mean you want the job?"

"Yes, ma'am." Sue turned to her son and laughed.

"Seems like all this girl's got in her is "Yes, ma'am." She turned back to me and smiled.

"You can start now by washing the pans, cleaning the mixer and mopping up in the kitchen. When you get that done, be here in the morning at six. My son, Albert, which I guess you already knew he was my son, since he yelled out at the top of his lungs, 'Mama!' Albert will teach you how to make the sandwiches and work the counter. You got a place to stay yet?"

"No, ma'am."

"Ah. They never do. I'll make some calls and see if there's someplace that'll put you up for the night. If I have to pay for your night's boarding it'll come out of your first check. Clear?"

"Yes, ma'am. Thank you. Do I need a uniform?" Sue looked at her son and began to giggle.

"No, dear. No uniforms or waitress dresses here. You're not going to be waiting tables. We dress casual, come as you are. You look clean enough. I'll provide an apron for you daily and two sandwiches and all the soda or sweet tea you can drink. Just be ready to work your ass off for me."

I worked through the day cleaning the kitchen. Sue came and went, restocking the shelves in the kitchen pantry without a word or a glance in my direction. At four that afternoon she called me upfront to the counter and motioned to one of the stools.

"Have a seat. The kitchen looks good. You've managed to impress me on your first day. Did you stop for lunch today?"

"No, ma'am."

"Albert! Nobody works through lunch. Make her a sandwich!" Sue sat down next to me, reached into her apron pocket and pulled out a slip of paper.

"You're in luck. A friend of mine owns an old two-story Victorian six blocks from here. She converted it into a boarding house about twenty years ago. She's got one vacancy. It's not the Ritz, just one small furnished room with a sink and toilet. I talked her into throwing in a hotplate and saucepan for you. That way you could boil an egg for breakfast and heat up a can of soup or hash for dinner."

Sue handed me the slip of paper. "There's her name and address. You can go now. We'll see you in the morning. And by the way, Miss Margie is a dear old friend of mine, Larraine, so you respect her house."

Miss Margie was older than Sue. She was on the front porch when I arrived, sitting in a bentwood rocker, a book in her hand, reading through thick hornrimmed glasses. She greeted me like an old friend, ushering me down the entrance hall and up the stairs, proudly telling me the history of the old house and the generations of her family who were born and lived out their lives within its walls. As she spoke she pointed out family portraits along the wall of the staircase. Her movements were genteel and her voice sweet and dripping like southern honeysuckle. Upstairs, when we reached the second door on the left down the hall, she stopped, turned to me and put a key in my hand.

"Well now, that's enough of my reflections on the past. Here's your room key. That's all you'll need. The front door is always unlocked. You go get yourself settled in, honey, and if you need me my quarters are downstairs in the very back. God bless and goodnight to you."

I put the key in the lock, turned it and opened the door to my freedom. The room was about the same size as the bedroom I shared with Cordie on the farm. There was a single wrought-iron bed with big fluffy pillows and a brilliant blue chenille bedspread. Beside it was a small oak table and a lamp with a fringed shade. There was also a standing wardrobe for clothes and a small sideboard holding the promised hotplate and saucepan. To the right a toilet and pedestal sink had been installed in a large closet. Two floor-to-ceiling windows were along the outer wall of the room. They were hung with heavy drapes in the same brilliant blue color as the bedspread. In front of the windows was a ladder-back chair where one could sit and see Miss Margie's rose garden below.

I was exhausted from the past two days and looking forward to a peaceful good night's sleep, but found myself leaving the bed to walk about the room, touching the furniture to make sure my freedom was real. From the room next door I could hear the faint strains of music from a static radio. It was late when I finally drifted into sleep.

The next day Albert patiently walked me through how to make the sandwiches. It was a lot to take in. By the end of the day I still had trouble remembering the names of the sandwiches and what went on them. As I left for the day Albert handed me a menu.

"I had trouble learning it too. Take this menu home and read it over and over. That's how I learned. Before you know it, you'll be making all these sandwiches like you've been doing it all your life. Least, that's what Mama always says."

Albert was right. Within two weeks all the combinations came easy. Albert didn't talk much but I grew to really like him and his quiet unspoken sense of humor. On days when sales didn't go well at the deli or the mixer or walk-in cooler failed, Albert would warn me to be prepared for his mama going on a tear. When Sue did just that, cursing, ranting and threatening to close the damn place down, Albert would make the funniest faces behind her back. Sue never caught him at it. I always had to turn away not to burst into laughter. We worked well together.

Jan Fink

TWELVE

Through the summer I worked the deli counter alongside Albert and spent my evenings with Miss Margie on the porch. Sometimes she'd tell stories about her family, how her grandfather was run down and killed by a buggy just down the street when the team of horses pulling it got spooked. And how two of her mother's sisters died in childbirth in one of the upstairs rooms. Most nights we just sat and read the many books she shared with me. My time with Miss Margie listening to her stories reminded me of the evenings on the porch with Cordie and Otha.

Coming home one late afternoon there was an old bicycle in the front yard. Its red and white paint was faded with chips of rust showing through but the tires looked new. There was a large basket attached to the handle bars and a bell. Hanging from the bell were six red roses tied up with kitchen twine. Miss Margie was on the porch peeling apples.

"You're running a little late today. Come up and sit with me for a while."

"Yes, ma'am. We were really busy at the deli."

"Hand me another apple out of that basket. I've had a powerful desire for an apple cobbler all day. You like apple cobblers?"

"Yes, ma'am, I do." I handed her the apple and she began peeling it, then shook her head.

"I've got plenty of apples but I'm not sure if I've got enough sugar. You never know how tart apples can be this time of year. Not enough sugar would make for a poor cobbler."

"I could go get sugar for you."

Miss Margie smiled. "You know how to ride a bicycle?"

"Yes, ma'am."

She pointed to the bicycle in the front yard. "So I guess you could ride that bicycle down the street and fetch me some sugar."

"Sure. That's a neat old bicycle!"

Miss Margie laughed. "Honey, it is old but that there is the Cadillac of bicycles. It's a Schwinn! Heavy and built to last, not like the cheap garbage they sell today. It's been out in the back shed for years. Belonged to my nephew. There used to be a little corner grocery store, but its long been gone. He worked there delivering groceries, pedaling that bicycle up and down the streets of this neighborhood all day."

She paused, looking out toward the street.

"That old Schwinn has been stored for more years than I can remember. I had my neighbor boy that cuts my grass get it out of the shed, clean it up as best he could and put new tires on it. He grumbled the whole time he was fixing it up, telling me I'd be better off going out and buying a new one. That's the way it is with young people these days. If it's broke, don't fix it, go buy a new one. He doesn't have any appreciation for old things. I didn't have a bow to put on it so I got the boy to cut some roses and tie them to the bell. Lord, did he complain. A couple of pinpricks from the rose thorns and you would have thought he was going to bleed to death. Between me and you, that boy is a bit lazy and close to becoming worthless."

"Should I go for your sugar now?" Miss Margie reached out and took my hand.

"Not just yet, honey. Me, my feeble old mind and mouth lost track of where I was going with this conversation. The reason I had the boy put the roses on it is I want to strike up a deal with you. I have my groceries delivered from the Piggly Wiggly and they charge me ten dollars a week. So I got to thinking a better use for that ten dollars a week might be that you could fetch my groceries and earn the money. And you could use the Schwinn to go back and forth to work and any other place you had a need to go. In other words, the bicycle is yours."

I lowered my head. Miss Margie leaned toward me. "What's wrong, honey? Oh, my word, are you crying? You are crying! You don't have to make the deal! Just forget about that old Schwinn and fetching my groceries."

"No, Miss Margie, I want the bicycle and to be of help to you. I'm crying because I'm happy and thankful for your kindness. You, Sue and Albert have been so nice to me. I'm not used to kindness. Thank you, so much."

"Honey, surely there has to have been someone in your life before you came here that was kind to you."

"Yes, ma'am. A few people."

"Well, now you've got me, Sue and Albert. You think you can dry your eyes and fetch me the sugar for my cobbler? Wouldn't do for you to take off crying and wreck that fine old Schwinn and bust my bag of sugar all over the road. You do that and I'll end up having to eat a bitter poor apple cobbler."

I tried to dry my eyes but the tears kept coming. Miss Margie reached into her apron pocket and handed me a handkerchief. True to her deep rooted southern style it was pressed linen with tiny embroidered red roses along the edges and the initial "M" in one corner.

"Stop your crying and go on now. I've almost got these apples peeled and I need that sugar."

I named the bicycle "Freedom" and together Freedom and I ran errands for Miss Margie and made the familiar trek to work and back home. Some days I ventured to other neighborhoods and found yard sales where I bought badly needed jeans, shirts, sneakers, boots and a hooded winter coat. I showed Miss Margie my yard sale finds.

"Honey, you did well. That coat looks almost brand new. But I've got to say that come winter you're going to need a little something more than that. We get a good many snow and ice storms up here. You take off on that Schwinn, get all covered with snow and darling you'll freeze over before you get down the street. Come on back to my quarters. I've got just the thing for you."

I'd never been inside Miss Margie's living area. It was like stepping into the past. The living room was filled with massive mahogany furnishings, heavy brocade drapes on the windows and thick oriental rugs. A grand piano stood in one corner, a fringed silk throw covered its top along with a half dozen photos in silver frames. In one photo a beautiful dark haired girl was playing the piano as a handsome young man leaned against it.

"Is this you, Miss Margie?"

Miss Margie picked up the frame and stared down at the photo.

"Yes, honey, that's me. I was the belle of the ball back then! 'Was,' is the key word here. That was a long time ago. Yes, I was the belle of the ball 'til I got hooked on petit fours and mint juleps. Do you play the piano?"

"No, ma'am."

"Well, I don't play anymore. Age and arthritis took my hands and made them crooked and the petit fours and mint juleps took my waist and made it thick. But enough about me, come on in the bedroom and I'll see if I can find that thing for you."

The bedroom was as beautiful as the living room. One entire wall consisted of nothing but a long closet in the same mahogany wood as the furnishings in the living room. It had six sets of double doors with handles made of porcelain. Miss Margie opened the left double doors and began thumbing through hangers of clothing.

"I'm sure it's still here. I never throw away anything. My mother was the same. Matter of fact, that far right closet is still full of her clothing. I've been told I could make a small fortune selling her clothes to the vintage clothing shop downtown. Course I never will because mother wouldn't like that. Ah, here it is. If my old eyes aren't deceiving me, I think this will fit you. Hard to believe I was about your size at one time. Honey, don't ever get hooked on petit fours and mint juleps. I'm a walking testimonial as to what they do to one's body."

Miss Margie handed me a hanger that held a clear plastic three-quarter length rain slicker with a belt and hood. I slipped it on. It was a perfect fit. Miss Margie smiled and patted my shoulder.

"That's going to work. It's old looking, but that was the style back then. When the snow and sleet come you wear that over your winter jacket while riding the Schwinn and you won't freeze up like a snowman."

"Thank you so much, Miss Margie. It's really cool. I wish it would snow tomorrow so I could wear it."

"Oh, my word! Let's get through the end of summer and fall before you go wishing for snow, honey!"

Jan Fink

THIRTEEN

With the beginning of fall came the festivals. We worked every festival that fall, getting up at three in the morning to load the refrigerated truck. Sue drove the truck to the fairgrounds with me and Albert in the seat beside her. They were long days but Sue was happy and grateful for the extra income the events provided. She was already searching catalogs for a new commercial mixer. Said the one she had now was just beat the hell to death and a new one would save her a lot of repair bills and cussing.

When the trees dropped their leaves Sue purchased a small hot table and added chili, beef stew and cornbread to the menu. She charged one dollar for a bowl of chili or stew with cornbread on the side. Albert told me she often gave it to the homeless for free.

After the lunch rush she called me to the kitchen. As kind as Sue was her shouting out in that raspy voice always intimidated me and made me fear that I'd done something wrong. Sue was a woman of few words and a combination of love and hate and anger all wrapped up together in her small stocky body. You never really knew if she liked, loved or hated you.

The kitchen was filled with the smell of simmering beef stock and tomatoes. Two large wooden chopping boards were on the work table along with a mound of fresh onions, bell peppers, carrots and potatoes. Sue handed me a large knife and motioned to the chopping board on the left.

"I need you back here for the rest of the day. I hope you're good with a knife. Albert is useless when it comes to chopping vegetables. He'd just as soon throw a whole onion, bell pepper and potato in the pot. Like that would make for a good stew!"

I took my place next to Sue. We worked in silence. For half an hour we chopped and transferred vegetables to the three big pots simmering on the stove. Sue brought more vegetables from the cooler, picked up her knife then paused, turning to me.

"You like living at Miss Margie's?"

"Oh, yes ma'am. She's really nice."

"Yes, she is. Are you making it and getting enough to eat on what I pay you? You look a little thin.

"I'm doing great. No matter how much I eat or don't eat, I stay thin."

Sue smiled and began chopping again. This time when she spoke her voice was softer.

"When I first came to Saint Florian I was two months pregnant with Albert, single and so poor and hungry that I went to every free event that served food and ate my fill. I ate my fill and while no one was looking I stuffed my purse and pockets with food. There was one night when I got home and I pulled a piece of cold chicken from my purse that it hit me as to how pathetic my life was. I swore to myself that my life was going to change. For the next seven months of my pregnancy I worked every job I could find. When Albert was born I walked the streets holding him on one hip and balancing a sample case on the other, selling cosmetics.

It took me ten years of working my ass off to make that change in my life and get this deli open, but look around, I've never been hungry since. Once a year on Christmas day I open these doors to the hungry. All they can eat for free. There's more people coming every year. Last year I fed five hundred homeless and hungry souls. Have you ever thought about what you want to do with your life? Do you have goals?"

"My one and only goal has always been freedom."

"Larraine, when you first came to me for work you said you were a runner and a lost soul. I'm not going to get heavy or deep with you by asking questions as to why you're a runner, feel your soul is lost or why you seek nothing more than freedom. But I do have one question. Is there anyone back there from where you came that loved and cared for you?"

"Yes, ma'am. My grandparents."

"Have you let them know that you're here and doing okay?"

"No, ma'am."

"Well, you can take my opinion or throw it away. If they were good to you and loved you, they must be heartbroken by now not knowing where or how you are. At the least I think you owe them a letter to ease their minds."

For the next week I thought about the letter. I loved and missed Cordie and Otha but at the same time I feared letting them know where I was. My biggest fears were that Daddy and the blue devils would find me and take me back home or James Lee would come to silence me. The second week I bought paper and pen and wrote and re-wrote a letter over and over, trying to explain my reasons for leaving. I finally decided to send nothing more than a short note telling Cordie and Otha that I loved them and I was okay. That I left to get away from

George and Ruby and to please not tell anyone where I was. I knew Cordie and Otha would honor that request.

It was a month before I heard back from Cordie. She wrote that she and Otha missed me but she knew I was okay because she'd had a dream. In the dream she could see me riding a thing with wheels and it was as red in color as my first horse, Dynamite. I was riding fast with my hair flowing back in the wind. There was other news from home. Two months after I left Little Brother quit school and left home also. Cordie said he had gone west looking for work. Ruby and George remained the same but Ruby was now talking about divorce. Cordie said she didn't believe in divorce but in their case it might be the best thing for both of them. In the closing lines of her letter she added that she feared Otha's health was failing and that he no longer was able to work as a watchman at the dump. She promised not to tell anyone where I was or that she'd heard from me and she asked me to think on the good.

Over the next six months Cordie and I wrote back and forth. Her letters were filled with descriptions of the harsh winter, spring planting and harvest time. Then her letters stopped coming. For three months I wrote to her weekly with no replies. The first week of the fourth month a letter from her finally arrived.

As Cordie had feared, Otha's decline in health had escalated. He had developed phlebitis in both legs and could no longer walk behind the plow from sun-up to sun-down. They had sold the mules, old half-blind Maud and Big Frank, and the plows that they had pulled up and down the rows for so many years. Cordie had made a small garden plot next to the farmhouse where she planted seeds for vegetables and worked the ground with her hoe. She'd also taken a part-time job as a lunchroom worker at the local school. They allowed her to bring leftover food home and with her small garden she said they would never go hungry. But she admitted that times were hard for her and Otha. The last paragraph of her letter took me to my knees.

Larraine, I've never asked for help from nobody and never thought I'd have a need to. But I don't like leaving Otha alone while I work at the lunchroom. It's looking like I may have to put in more hours working in the lunchroom and also doing janitor work at the school to make ends meet. I'm ashamed to say it but I need help with the garden and such too. Poor folks have poor ways. Could ya come home and help me for a spell? Ya wouldn't have to go back to living with Ruby and George. Ya could live here with me and Otha. Ya a grown woman now and ya can live where ya want to. Don't worry about Ruby and George trying to take ya out of my house. They do and I'll take a fire poker to 'em. If ya can come, let me know and I'll put back some money to help ya with bus fare. We love ya, Cordie

How could I go back? How could I give up freedom? How could I not give up freedom? How could I not go back to help Cordie and Otha? They had given me light and laughter and love in the midst of a dark childhood. For two weeks I went back and forth, undecided. So much went through my mind. If I went back I could ignore James Lee and never be alone with him. If Daddy and the blue devils showed up at the farm, Cordie would protect me. In the end, my heart told me I had to go.

I wrote back, telling Cordie I was coming home to her and Otha. It would be two weeks, maybe a month before I could leave. I had to give notice at my job and tie up loose ends and there was no need for her to send money for bus fare. I asked only that she not tell anyone just yet that I was coming. I would be in touch and let her know my arrival date and time and hoped she could meet me at the bus depot.

I knew the hardest part would be giving Sue my notice. She had been the major key to my freedom. So I waited two days after posting the letter to Cordie to approach Sue. At the end of my shift that day I called Sue aside and asked if we could talk. She stood impatient as always, wiping her hands on her apron, ready for quick conversation so she could get back to her kitchen.

"Well? What? I've got bread coming out of the oven in about five minutes."

I mumbled, "I have to go."

"Go where? Somebody offered you a new job making more money? Is this your way of asking me for a raise to keep you on?"

"No, ma'am! It's not that at all!"

"Then what is it?"

"I have to go home."

"So you're telling me that you're running back to the very thing you ran from?"

"I have to."

"My bread is close to being done. I'll ask you one more time. Why do you have to go?"

"My grandparents need me. I'll stay 'til you can find someone else to take my place."

Sue's face and demeanor softened.

"I understand." Then she turned to Albert and shouted, "Put the help wanted sign in the window."

She went back to the kitchen without another word. Albert put the sign in the window and turned to me. "Don't be upset. Mama really likes you. That's just her way of dealing with people and things. She's got a good heart." Then he made one

214

of his frowny, angry Sue imitation faces and touched his heart with his right hand.

There were a lot of applicants. Sue interviewed them quickly and just as quickly sent them on their way. One was too old and slow and would never be able to keep up with the lunch hour rush. Three giggled and talked too much. One was as surly looking as a bulldog and another smelled like a wet collie. Worst of all, Sue said that at least a half dozen of them didn't know the difference between a slice of roast beef and a slice of pastrami.

It was two weeks before Sue found a suitable applicant. A small heavy-set young girl of German lineage that knew the meats and moved quickly despite her size. Her name was Mary and she was as shy and quiet as Albert. With a little help from me and Albert, within a week Mary was working the counter like a pro. Sue told me I was free to go and make plans for my trip home. And to let her know the day before I was to leave and she'd bring my week's pay over to Miss Margie's.

The next morning I booked a ticket for the coming Saturday and wrote to Cordie that I'd be arriving around four that afternoon. The rest of the week I narrowed down my clothing to what would fit in the same backpack I'd arrived with in Saint Florian. I was surprised that I'd accumulated so much. I saved out the rain slicker to give back to Miss Margie, then filled the basket of the Schwinn with the rest and donated them to a thrift store. That last week, I rode the streets daily on the old Schwinn that I called Freedom. There were so many things and people that I hated leaving behind.

The evening before departing Miss Margie asked me to come to her quarters. Sue and Albert were there. Miss Margie had set up a card table and covered it with a lace tablecloth. There was a large pitcher of iced tea and a platter filled with beautiful little decorated cakes of all colors. Miss Margie gave me a big hug, took my hand and led me to the table.

"Nobody leaves my house without a little going away party. And don't you go crying on me, honey."

Then she looked at Sue and Albert. "Don't know if you two have noticed but this girl cries at the slightest show of kindness. Larraine, these are those petit fours I told you about. Every young southern lady should experience a petit four at least once in life. I think I'll splurge today and have one myself. But, just one. Like I told you, Larraine, petit fours and I have a history. Surely just one won't hurt and hopefully I'll be spared getting hooked on the little devil cakes again. The blue ones are my favorite. Now come on everyone and help yourself."

We ate the little cakes and talked. They didn't ask questions about the home I was going back to. I volunteered stories about Cordie and Otha's farm and my childhood there. Having been city dwellers, Miss Margie, Sue and Albert were amazed by the stories of simple farm life.

When the last of the petit fours were gone we said our goodbyes. Sue gave me my weeks' pay and a brief tap on the arm.

"If you ever have the need to be a runner again, I hope you run this way. I can always use a good, hard worker. Good luck to you, Larraine."

"Thank you, ma'am. Thank you for everything."

Albert stepped forward, his head down, moving his right foot back and forth across the thick oriental carpet. He stood that way 'til Sue cleared her throat and shouted.

"Dammit Albert! Get on with it! She's got to catch a bus in the morning!"

Albert raised his head and reached into his pocket. He pulled out a piece of folded paper and gave it to me.

"That's our menu. It's got our address at the top. Maybe you could write me sometime and tell me how things are going for you. I think it would be fun to have a pen pal."

"Thank you, Albert. I'd love to be pen pals with you."

He smiled and shook my hand like we were sealing a deal, then stepped back behind Sue. Last to say goodbye was Miss Margie.

"I'm going to miss our chats and reading together on the porch. I've enjoyed having you in my home."

"I've enjoyed my stay with you, Miss Margie. Especially all the great stories you've told me about this town, this house and your family. Tonight I'll return the rain slicker you loaned me. Most of all, thank you for letting me use the Schwinn."

"Oh, honey, you keep that rain slicker. I'm sure that where you're going there will be a little rain, maybe even snow and sleet. Besides, thanks to the petit fours and mint juleps, I'll never get my thick body in that slicker again. You're welcome to it. As to the Schwinn, I'm going to get that worthless neighbor boy to put it back in the shed. Who knows, like Sue said, you might just run this way again. Hopefully that old Schwinn and I will be right here waiting for you."

With that last goodbye my brief freedom ended and come morning the bus would take me to another life chapter at home.

Jan Fink

Cordie was waiting at the depot as promised. She looked tired and thinner than the last time I saw her. We greeted with hugs, tears and kisses on the cheek.

"Larraine, I'm so glad ya came. I hate to hurry but I didn't have nobody to stay with Otha. Mr. Fields from the grocery drove me to town. He's waiting in the truck over there. He needs to get back to his store so we best not keep him waiting."

I was immediately uncomfortable. Mr. Fields knew everyone in the community and I wondered if he had told anyone I was coming home. We started the drive to the farm. Cordie pointed out the changes along the way. A house that burned to the ground and another torn down and replaced with a gas station. Halfway home Mr. Fields asked Cordie if she needed to pick up anything before we reached the outskirts of town. Cordie told him no, she was in a hurry to get home to Otha. Then he spoke to me.

"Larraine, I want to ease your mind about things. I ain't told nobody about you coming home and don't plan to. Especially your daddy. He still comes in my store often, buying beer and cigarettes. Every time he shows up he's more messed up than the last time. So, don't worry about me telling him or nobody else nothing. That's your business. But, Larraine, you're smart enough to know that sooner or later word's gonna get out about you being back. It's a small community and everybody knows everybody else's business."

"Thank you, Mr. Fields. And thank you for bringing Cordie to the depot to pick me up."

Mr. Fields was right. I couldn't hide forever. But I did hope for as much time as possible alone with Cordie and Otha 'til that day came. Cordie asked Mr. Fields to let us off at the top of the lane. She thanked him, took my hand and we walked toward the farmhouse. The fields on both sides of the lane held no crops. They were overgrown with knee high weeds. The foot of the big oak in the front yard where Otha always parked his truck was now piled waist high with tin cans.

"Cordie, where's Dawkins?" For a moment she looked puzzled, then smiled.

"Oh, ya mean Otha's old truck. I'd forgot that's what he called it. Don't know why he called it Dawkins. Otha give a nickname to everything and everybody he loved. He called me his blue eyes, but never in front of nobody. That wouldn't a been proper. While ya was gone, when we sat on the porch in the evenings, he'd tap his foot and say to me, "Reckon where our Bitterweed is tonight?

"I don't remember Otha ever calling me Bitterweed."

"He didn't. That was speaking tween me and him in private. He started calling ya Bitterweed cause he was fraid all that stuff 'tween Ruby and George was turning ya heart yellow. He worried about ya all the time and missed ya."

"I'm really sorry that I didn't write to you and Otha sooner. I'm glad to be back home with you."

"I'm glad ya back. Anyways, bout the old truck, do ya remember when he used to pick ya up for weekends. Ya granddaddy never even had a driver's license but he bought that truck off who he thought was a friend. But he weren't no friend to Otha far as I thought, taking Otha's hard earned money for such an excuse of a truck. The floorboard was half rotted out, no windshield wipers and the brakes wouldn't hold lest ya poured fluid in ever five miles. Every time he took off to town to pick ya up I worried something terrible 'til I saw y'all coming back down the lane safe. But, don't matter now. Otha's legs can't push the clutch, brake or gas pedal no more. I sold what was left of Dawkins to a boy in town for two hundred dollars. He was wanting to re-build it cause he said it was a classic. I wished him luck. That old truck weren't nothing more than a classic mess far as I could tell. The money I got went to the doctor visits for Otha's legs."

"I asked Mr. Fields to drop us off at the top of the lane cause I wanted to talk to ya afore we get to the house. As ya can see, lots a things have been let go. Otha just ain't able no more. He's worse than when I wrote to ya and ask ya to come home. His poor old legs ain't fit for nothing these days. They can barely carry his weight."

"Is there no medicine or a doctor that can help him?"

"Larraine, if they was we still wouldn't have the money for it. Come right down to it, it's just old age and there ain't no magic pill for that. Nature and time gone do what it wants to do."

"I'm so sorry, Cordie."

"Ain't no need a being sorry. Old age comes to all of us sooner or later. I'm glad ya here. Ya gonna be a great comfort and help to me and Otha. And another thing I wanted to tell ya, Larraine, is lately, Otha's thoughts wander sometimes. So if he says something out a sorts don't pay it no mind."

Halfway to the farmhouse I could hear the sound of yelping.

"Do you have a dog now, Cordie?"

"Yeah, a big old red bone hound. He showed up out a nowhere not long after ya left. Poor thing was half starved, mangy and covered in ticks. He's half blind in one eye and half lame in one leg. We cleaned him up and put some weight back on him. He stays right by Otha's side. Otha thinks he might a been somebody's hunting dog at one time and when he got too old to hunt they threwed him out on the road. Otha said it was a pity that somebody would treat an old dog like that so he named him Pity."

When we neared the porch Otha began to wave, Pity by his side with his tail wagging.   Otha yelled out.

"Larraine, Larraine! Ya come home at last!"

I ran to him and hugged him tightly. "Yes! Otha, I'm home! Cordie tells me this is Pity. Can I pet him? Does he bite?"

"Yeah, ya can pet him. That old hound ain't hardly got enough teeth in his head to eat, much less try and bite anybody."

Cordie smiled and some of the weariness left her face. "Ya stay out here on the porch with Otha and catch up while I fry us a piece a ham for supper. Gonna be light eating tonight."

I sat with Otha and told him stories about the deli where I worked and all the different kinds of breads, meat, vegetables and cheeses we used. He'd never heard of a meat called pastrami or swiss or provolone cheese. He had a lot of questions.

"Ya mean that a body could walk in that place where you worked and get a sandwich with any of 'em meats or cheeses or vegetables on it?"

"Yes, sir. Any way you want it."

"That sounds like a fine place, Larraine. I think someday I'd like to go to one 'em places."

"So, how've you been, Otha?"

"I reckon Cordie told ya about my legs." He reached down and pulled up his pants legs. His legs were a red landscape, the veins blue and raised and knotty like the ridges of a mountain.

"Damn phlebitis stuff just sneaked up on me and seems to get worse ever day. I'm not much good for the fields or walking these days. I'm like an old spider that somebody done pulled two of its legs off. I just creep around."

"I'm sorry Otha about your legs. And I'm sorry I took off without saying goodbye to you and Cordie."

"Oh, we knowed ya weren't running from us. We did worry for a spell not knowing anything, hoping ya hadn't been kidnapped or something. Cordie told me about her dream and said she was sure ya was somewhere okay. What was that red thing on wheels ya was riding in her dream? Did ya have ya a car where you was?

"No, Otha. It was just a big old red bicycle I was riding."

"Now ain't that something. All this time I had a picture in my mind a ya riding around in a big red convertible car."

We had our evening meal on the porch that night. A big bowl of crumbled cornbread soaked in buttermilk and topped with big chunks of ham. Cordie called it a light supper but to me it was coming home to her and Otha.

We settled into a routine of work. Li'l Belle and a brood of fifty banty hens and roosters remained on the farm. When she returned each afternoon from work at the lunchroom, Cordie taught me how to milk Li'l Belle and churn the milk to make butter and buttermilk. She told me the best time of day to gather eggs from the banty hen's nest and how to fry the eggs in bacon grease and make biscuits and strong brewed coffee for Otha's breakfast. In the evening, as Otha and Pity watched from the porch we weeded her little garden and picked tomatoes, squash, okra and peas, and put them up in jars for the coming winter.

One day at dusk as Cordie and I harvested the last of the vegetables we heard Pity yelping. A black pick-up truck was slowly making its way down the lane toward the farmhouse.

"Who is that, Cordie?"

"James Lee. He don't ride horses much anymore. Got his self a truck now. He comes by at least once a month. Says he comes to check up on me and Otha. He always ask if we heard any news about ya. He's gone be happy to see ya."

I had been so content being back with Cordie and Otha the past few months I had rarely thought of James Lee. The few times I did, I knew that eventually our paths would cross. I also knew that this time I couldn't run. James Lee was at the edge of the porch talking to Otha. Then he turned and looked toward the garden and fell silent. Cordie picked up the two baskets of vegetables and handed one to me.

"Come on, Larraine. We've got enough of what's left of the tomatoes to keep us busy the next couple a days."

We walked toward the porch and by halfway there I could already see a big smile on James Lee's face. He closed the gap between us, walking quickly the last few yards, then threw his arms around me, picking me up, whirling me around in a circle like we were long lost lovers. I tried to put distance between me and him with the basket of vegetables but he just held on tighter. I felt dizzy and nauseous and at the same time a feeling of such hatred toward him rose from my stomach to the back of my throat like bile. He finally released me and stepped back, looking me up and down.

"Larraine, Larraine! Where have you been, girl?"

"Just away for a while, James Lee."

"Well, come on up to the porch and sit next to me. We've got some catching up to do."

James Lee sat down on the porch swing and patted the wooden seat next to him. I took a seat in one of the rockers between Cordie and Otha. James Lee kept smiling and talking.

"Got to say, Larraine, you're looking good. Ain't she Miss Cordie and Otha? Ain't she looking good?" No one spoke.

"Tell me what you've been up to. I want to hear everything. Where you've been? Who you've been with? What have you been doing all these many months you've been away? Come on. Don't keep me in suspense."

"Out of town for a while, that's all, James Lee."

"Ah, now. That ain't fair, Larraine."

Otha looked annoyed and cleared his throat, then turned to James Lee.

"What's with all the questions? Ya working for channel 6 news now? Larraine done told ya all she wants to tell ya."

James Lee kept on smiling, looking past Otha to me.

"Ain't nothing wrong about being curious, is there, Otha? But, you know, I do seem to remember Larraine never did talk much. Ain't that right, Larraine? You don't talk much or share much with other folks, do you?"

Again, no one spoke. Cordie broke the silence. "James Lee, we had a good crop of tomatoes this year. I'll go in and put some in a basket for ya to take to your mama."

"My mama would greatly appreciate that, Miss Cordie."

Cordie went inside and we in sat silence. James Lee was still staring at me. The only sound was the creaking of the porch swing. Finally James Lee spoke again.

"How do you like my new truck, Larraine? It's fully loaded, even has real leather seats. Come on, I'll take you for a ride."

Otha answered for me. "She ain't got time for no ride. Her and Cordie got to get working on putting up tomatoes. Nice of ya to come by James Lee."

"No problem, Otha. I can take Larraine for that ride another time. Now that I know she's back I'll be coming by more often."

Otha watched the lane 'til the truck pulled onto the highway then turned to me.

"Larraine, is James Lee sweet on ya?"

"I hope not."

"Well, I'm glad to hear that. Like I done told ya afore I don't trust him. Ever since he got that truck he got his self a lot more attitude. And ever time he comes by here I smell whiskey on his breath. He ain't nobody ya would ever want to hook-up with."

"You don't have to worry about that, Otha. I really don't want anything to do with him."

Cordie came back to the porch carrying the basket of tomatoes. "Why'd he leave without his mama's tomatoes?"

"Cause I politely give him the hint to leave, Cordie. He was wanting to take Larraine for a ride in his truck. Sitting here eyeballing her right in front of me on my own front porch. And putting pressure on her to tell him all her business. And I knowed he'd been hitting the whiskey afore he got here. He comes back around again I want ya and Larraine to stay in the house. I don't want him coming round here no more and next time he does I'll make that clear to him."

Cordie and I promised to do as Otha asked.

FIFTEEN

It was three weeks later while Cordie and I were at the lean-to milking and feeding Li'l Belle that we heard Pity's yelps and loud voices coming from the farmhouse. Cordie dropped the feed bucket she was holding and grabbed my arm. "Oh, Lord! Larraine, I betcha James Lee's come back."

I knew what James Lee was capable of. I was afraid for Otha. My first thought was to run to the farmhouse, but before I could take a step Cordie tightened her grip on my arm and shook her head and said, no.

"Stay right here, Larraine. Remember what Otha said. He don't want me and ya to be around James Lee. Otha knows what he's doing. Let him handle this on his own."

For five minutes the loud yelling continued, then we heard the sound of James Lee's truck tires slinging gravel and speeding down the lane. Otha was outside on the porch when Cordie and I reached the farmhouse. His face was red and beaded with sweat. Cordie ran to him, taking his hand.

"Are ya okay, Otha? He didn't raise his hand to ya, did he?"

"I'm okay, Cordie. If he'd a raised his hand to me, I'd a killed him. He comes back here again I may just have to kill him. I can't stand too well on my legs but I can damn sure sit in a chair and hold a shotgun. Larraine, go to the well and draw me up some cool water. All that hollering got me heated up and dry mouthed."

I went to the well. As I dropped the bucket and pulled it back up my knees were shaking. I wanted James Lee gone. Really gone. I wanted him dead.

"Otha, afore Larraine comes back, what was all the yelling about? What did he say to get ya so mad?"

"Weren't so much what he said, Cordie. There's something wrong with him. That's all I'm gone tell ya. Ya got to promise me that when I leave this earth, ya will keep him away from Larraine."

For weeks the sound of an engine along the highway at the end of the lane brought us to attention. We watched the lane in fear that it would be James Lee coming back. His truck passed by on the highway often, its horn blaring, but he never turned down the lane to the farmhouse. We never spoke of him but the tension and fear of his returning was always there between us.

In the fall Cordie stopped working at the school lunchroom. With Otha in bad health it took me and Cordie both to care for the farm animals and tend the garden. We planted turnip and mustard greens, radishes and green onions. As we tended the garden next to the farmhouse Otha would call out to us.

"Cordie, check to be sure the greens ain't been took over by cutworms. Won't be a leaf a greens left if 'em worms get a hold of 'em."

Cordie and I would call out together, "The greens are fine, Otha." Then Otha would call out again.

"Cordie, ya and Larraine watching for snakes? Ya know they ain't gone to sleep for the winter yet. And a snake just loves to hide up under a nice stand of greens."

It was torture for Otha to have to watch from the porch as we worked. He missed being in the fields and behind the plow. Coming in from the garden one evening Cordie stopped me before we reached the porch.

"Larraine, it's been nearly a year since Otha told a story. I don't know if it's the pain in his legs that keeps him quiet or if he ain't got no more stories to tell. And lately this thing with James Lee seems to have taken his voice and his wind. See if ya can get him to tell us a story tonight."

"I noticed that too. I'll try, Cordie."

Through supper I tried to think of a subject that might get Otha telling a story. From my earliest memories he'd never been a church goer, but he did attend funerals and helped with grave digging. Every year before Cordie's church had Decoration Day, Otha would hitch a ride to the cemetery and take me and Little Brother along with him. He'd bring along hoes for each of us and we'd clear away weeds. I remember him tossing the old plastic grave arrangements down the sloping hill at the rear of the cemetery. The colors of the newly tossed plastic flowers on top of arrangements from years before were more vibrant. To me and Little Brother that slope looked like a cartoon land. A magic sloping hill of all colors and shapes that we were sure led down through the pines to a magical castle. We would beg Otha to let us go down and explore and play among the plastic flowers. His answer was always the same. "No! That ain't nothing but a good bed for rattlers!"

Those trips to the cemetery were as close as Otha came to church going. I had not attended a church since the days of Ruby finding and then losing interest in religion. Since the mock saving and baptism that had been forced on me years ago, if Jesus truly was out there I'd yet to find him. I was curious to see if Otha held the same opinion on religion as I did so that evening I asked him.

"Otha, you've always helped out at Cordie's church. I'm curious as to why you don't go to church services."

"Funny, ya would ask me about that. While I was watching ya and Cordie cleaning the weeds out of the garden today I got to thinking about Decoration Day. I don't reckon I'll be of any use helping with this next one coming up. I also got to thinking that that's the graveyard I want to be put in when the time comes."

Cordie moaned and for the first time she raised her voice to Otha. "Ya hush now, Otha! Ya got to think on the good."

"Cordie, I got to think on what's coming. Be it good or bad. Only a fool don't have a plan. It's time for me to make a plan. That graveyard at your church is where I want to be planted and Cordie, I want the lid to my box shut down. I don't want nobody standing over me crying like they just found a good hog froze to the ground in winter afore they could put it in the smokehouse."

Cordie put her hands to her face and again cried out, "Stop this talk now! I can't abide it!"

Otha didn't answer her, but looked to me. "Larraine, ya got yourself saved when ya was little, didn't ya?"

"The church told me I was saved. At the time I didn't understand what I was being saved from. To this day I don't really feel that I was saved from anything."

"I ain't never been saved neither. And don't see the need in it now. But I think they'll still plant me in the ground over there at Cordie's church."

"So Otha, you don't believe in Jesus?"

"Ah, Larraine, I ain't saying I don't believe in Jesus. I believe in many things but preachers or "men of the calling" ain't one of 'em. They just men like me. Some of 'em ain't got as much sense as this old hound Pity laying at my feet. They take what's writ in the Bible and twist it to suit their own purpose. That don't seem like no kind of good calling in my book." He smiled, then laughed and began to tap his feet on the porch floor.

"I'll tell ya a story about my younger days and how I came close to getting mixed up with a preacher. Ya remember that preacher, don't ya, Cordie?"

"Now Otha, that ain't no fit story to be telling a young girl."

"Cordie, Larraine's old enough and I think she needs to hear it and learn from it. Sides, she seems to have the same opinion as me when it comes to religion."

"Well, Larraine, back in the early days when me and Cordie first married she did her best to get me through the doors of her church. Larraine, she tried everything from sweet talk to the threat of hell's fire and brimstones in the hope of seeing me on a pew come Sunday morning. There was a brief time when I came awful close to giving in. In those days the church had rotating preachers. They'd come and go pretty much with the change of seasons.

One fall a new preacher arrived and he made his self pretty popular with all the womenfolk. In no time at all he'd made such an impression on the ladies that most of us menfolk found our lives being made miserable. That preacher had all the womenfolk stirred up worse than a stepped on, foot high fire ant bed. They were determined to get everyone of us men in church. It all sorta happened gradually. Cordie invited that new preacher to our house for Sunday dinner. I didn't object cause my curiosity was up about this man of the calling and his hold on all the womenfolk. Well, when he arrived I understood part of the womenfolk's excitement. He did talk good and was fair to look at."

"So he was handsome?"

"I reckon ya could call him that, Larraine. He had his hair all slicked back and was wearing a fine new suit and tie. Of course Cordie asked him to say the blessing. And that's when my first complaint came about. He just talked and talked and his blessing went on 'til my eyes were beginning to cross and the fried chicken on my plate was stone cold. I do believe he would have gone on 'til the next Sunday with that blessing if I hadn't cut him short by saying, "God Bless and Amen!"

Otha leaned forward in his chair and laughed. Cordie gave out a grunt and turned her head away, looking out at the fields. "I was never more embarrassed in my life!"

"I had to do something, Cordie. I was hungry. Anyway, the preacher was real fond of holding prayer visits. He'd set 'em up at a different church member's home once a week. I put my foot down and told Cordie I didn't want one of 'em at our house. But that didn't spare me the company of that long-winded preacher. Our nearest neighbor, he give in and allowed the preacher to have the next prayer visit at his home. I guess his wife had harped on him 'til he finally said yes, just to shut her up. So when Cordie asked me to go with her I said yes for the same reason. To keep peace and stop her from harping.

There were about eight of us in attendance that night. The neighbor's wife had made three dozen fried apple pies and a big pot of strong coffee. After we eat, the preacher called us to prayer. Winter was well set in, so we kneeled around the woodstove for warmth. The preacher took out his Bible and started praying. He started out at a low, slow pace. Then his words quickened and built up to an all-out screaming of the gospel. He was huffing and puffing out his words so hard that he was drawing smoke right out of the grate on the woodstove. That preacher's mouth worked better than any set of bellows I ever seen. The more he talked the hotter the fire in the woodstove got. The heat didn't seem to bother him. He just went on like he was totally filled by the spirit."

"I tried to keep my eyes shut, Larraine, but just like that Sunday dinner my eyes were beginning to cross under their lids and my legs were falling asleep from kneeling that long. The preacher was getting louder and more filled with the spirit by the minute. I decided to shift my legs a little and open my eyes and when I did, I saw the spirit that was filling up the preacher. I saw it so clear that I stood right up and shouted, Hallelujah! Amen! And ended the prayer visit, right there and then. The reason is that when I opened my eyes and looked over at the preacher, he had his hand on the leg of my neighbor's wife. Yep, that preacher was standing there holding a Bible in one hand and holding my neighbor's wife's leg in the other hand. Every time he raised his voice and puffed out his words he'd throw his head back and squeeze down harder on her leg.

Now, I got to tell ya I had no choice but to let my neighbor know and after that night the new preacher didn't stay long in the community. It was a long time afore any of the womenfolk harped on their husbands' about going to church again. Even Cordie stopped trying to get my foot in the church door. All I can say is that man of the calling brought about the brief beginning and end of my religious period."

I couldn't help but begin to laugh. Otha laughed with me, slapping his hands on the arms of his chair. Cordie gave in too, laughing and wiping her eyes with her apron.

SIXTEEN

It was to be the last story Otha told. Winter came early with heavy frost in the mornings and bitter cold temperatures at night. Men from Cordie's church cut loads of firewood, brought it to the farmhouse and stacked it outside the kitchen door for us. I carried armloads of the wood inside, putting it next to the big fireplace in the central room and in the kitchen by the woodstove. When freezing rain came I wore the clear plastic rain slicker over my winter coat as I carried the wood and thought of Miss Margie's words: 'I'm sure that where you're going there will be a little rain, maybe even snow and sleet'.

I brought the three rockers from the porch inside and we spent our evenings in front of the big fireplace. Some nights Otha would take the small fireplace shovel and rake the hot coals forward and we'd roast potatoes or a pan of peanuts on them. As the top of the coals began to turn to ash he stirred them 'til they glowed golden. He pointed to the coals and said, "Look there. I'm a rich man."

Cordie laughed and asked him how that could be. He pointed to the golden coals again.

"That's my gold right there, Cordie. And the best part is when it's gone I can always make more."

"Well, Otha, it's a good thing ya can make more cause that gold liable to burn a hole in ya pocket."

Every night we remained at the fireside 'til bedtime. The freezing rain continued for a week and the days and nights got even colder. No matter how much wood I fed the fire, we shivered. Dressed in our winter coats we pulled the rockers closer to the fire. Pity lay with his head on Otha's feet, sometimes snoring and grunting in his sleep. Otha had developed a deep raspy cough. It came in violent fits, taking his breath. He began taking to his bed early. Each night Cordie heated her sad irons in the hot coals of the fire, wrapped them in flour sacks and placed them at his feet. It gave Otha more warmth but the fits of coughing continued to grow worse. She made a mustard poultice, then went to the closet and pulled out one of Otha's flannel shirts.

"I hate to tear up clothes but this old shirt is more holy than righteous anyway. It'll do fine." She ripped out the back of the shirt, folded it and spread the poultice on it. It became a nightly routine of placing the sad irons at Otha's feet and the poultice on his chest. With that done she'd return to the fireside, take her Bible down from the fireplace mantel and read aloud.

By the next morning the freezing rain had turned to snow. It blanketed the fields and hung in big white clumps from the limbs of the pines at the edge of the woodland. The snow continued to fall, creating a quiet picturesque fairytale stillness about the farm. Cordie and I trudged through the snow to milk and feed Li'l Belle and to feed the chickens and gather their eggs. The second morning of snow we found six hens frozen on their nest along with their eggs.

"Larraine, this is a bad sign. A banty hen don't have a lot of sense. Some of 'em don't even come to the coop to build their nest and lay eggs. I've found nests in the yard and at the edge of the woodland. If this cold keeps up, we'll lose a lot more of 'em that we could put on the table along with their eggs. Them frozen eggs ain't no good now. Even if I was starving I couldn't bring myself to thaw out 'em hens, cook 'em and eat 'em cause of the way they died. We'll take 'em nests and all and throw 'em out in the fields. Some coyote and his family will make use of 'em."

Midafternoon Otha asked me to help him up and out onto the porch. He stood holding the porch post looking out over his farm.

"Now, Larraine, ain't that just about the prettiest thing ya ever saw?"

"Yes, it is. Are you sure you're warm enough? Maybe we should go back inside."

"In a minute. In my whole life I ain't ever seen but one other big snow like this. One of my old sows froze to death right over there in the field. I had to wait for the thaw to peel her up off of the ground. It was a hard time but that snow was just as pretty as this one. I just want to stand here and drink it in a little longer. How about ya go out in the yard and roll me up a couple a snowballs."

I brought the snowballs to Otha. He leaned against the porch post with his arms wrapped about it, a snowball in each hand and smiled.

"Now I want ya to go back out to the yard so I can throw these at ya."

Both throws hit me square in the chest. Otha threw back his head and began laughing, but the cold air and effort took his breath. A bad fit of coughing came on, his chest rattling in between the coughs. He gripped the porch post tightly and for a moment I was afraid his legs would give way. I called Cordie to help me get him inside and next to the fire. It was ten minutes before the coughing subsided, but the rattle in his chest remained and chills set in. Cordie covered him with quilts as I brought in more wood for the fire.

"Guess I got a mite chilled out there."

"Yes, ya did, Otha. Why in the world would ya want to get out of your sickbed and go out on the porch?"

"To see the snow, Cordie. To see that pretty snow. Ya remember that other big snow?"

"I do. Can't forget it. We like to froze to death."

"Cordie, my teeth are a trying to chatter on me. Tell Larraine about that other big snow."

"Well, the winter that year started out just like this one. Otha had cut wood off and on all the summer afore. When the snow came it didn't stop, it just kept coming and it got colder and colder. We kept the fireplace and woodstove burning day and night. Even when the snow finally stopped and began to thaw a little, it stayed cold and windy. Within a week or so we was running short on wood. Otha got worried and went to looking for anything we could burn to tide us over 'til he could get to the woodland to cut more trees.

Next thing I knowed he had broke up the kitchen table chairs and burnt 'em. Then he burnt the headboard of our bed. After that burned down he took all the closet doors off their hinges, chopped 'em up and throwed 'em on the fire. All that old dried up furniture and closet doors burned fast and hot like lighter pine. We were nice and warm one minute and back to freezing the next."

Cordie pointed to the fireplace mantel. "Larraine, I saw him eyeing the mantel there where I always keep my Bible. And the look in his eyes told me that was what he was fixing to tear down and burn next. I wasn't about to have that so I picked up the fire poker and stood 'tween him and the mantel."

"Cordie! Would you have really hit him with the poker?"

"Larraine, that's 'tween me and the Lord. But as ya can see, the mantel is still there and my Bible is still resting on it." Otha gave out a short laugh.

"Yep, Larraine. That was the worst spat me and Cordie ever had. But I was man enough to know ya don't come 'tween a woman with a fire poker and the resting place for her Bible. I'd just soon froze to death than to do that." He attempted to laugh again, but only a wheeze came out and he clutched his chest.

"Cordie, why don't ya take down that old wore out Bible a yours and read to me for a spell?"

"I'd be glad to Otha. Larraine, while I read would ya go out and bring in more wood to dry out for the fire?"

While Cordie read aloud I kept the fire stoked. From time to time Otha would pat his foot and say, "What ya really need, Larraine, is a big old back-stick to keep a fire burning all night long. Remember, Cordie, I used to be able to carry in a back-stick from the woodpile that was as big around as me and the fire would burn all night long."

He reached down and patted the old hound at his feet. The effort increased the rattle in his chest. He sighed. "I think I'm gonna lie down for a while afore supper. Sitting up like this ain't agreeing with my chest. Come on and let's go rest a while Pity."

Cordie and I put our arms around his waist and guided him to his bedroom. Pity weaved in and out between our legs, almost tripping us. We covered Otha with quilts. Cordie went back to the fireplace and put the sad irons on the coals to heat and place at his feet. Pity stood at his bedside looking up and whining 'til Otha reached out his hand and patted his head.

"Larraine, go tell Cordie to bring a quilt and put it on the floor next to the bed for Pity. I know that floor gotta be awful cold on his old bones." As I turned to leave the room Otha called out.

"Larraine, do ya remember what I taught ya about the bond 'tween human beings and four-leggers?"

"I remember everything you taught me, Otha."

"Good. Always show 'em respect. Old Pity come here to the farm for a reason. That being, we got to take care of him."

Cordie was in the kitchen making another mustard poultice and a pot of soup and cornbread for supper. I told her Otha asked for a quilt for Pity. She smiled and shook her head and then went to the wardrobe next to the fireplace and began pulling out quilts. She thumbed through them 'til she found the one she was looking for.

"This one is frayed round the edges and has a few holes in it but I guess it'll be good enough for a hound. In all my years with Otha I ain't never seen him take to a dog like this. Wouldn't even allow a dog in the house and here he is asking for a quilt on the floor for one. Pull 'em sad irons off the coals and wrap 'em up good. Careful not to burn yourself."

I wrapped the sad irons and followed Cordie to Otha's bedroom. We placed the hot irons at his feet then Cordie folded the quilt and placed it on the floor next to his bed. Pity circled the quilt and pawed it up into a lumpy pile before he finally laid down on it. Cordie grunted.

"Well, if that don't beat all. That old hound don't even give me the time of day and now I can't even make a fit bed according to him."

"He appreciates it, Cordie and so do I. He's a good old hound."

"He's a hound that's got ya wrapped around his paw. Why ya make over him so much, Otha?"

"Cause that old hound is the angel that's gonna take me to heaven."

Cordie looked at me. Her face showed amusement and alarm.

"What ya got on your mind, Otha? What ya thinking about?"

Otha smiled and pulled the quilts higher on his chest.

"I'm thinking on the good."

"Close ya eyes, Otha, and rest for a while. Supper will be ready in about an hour. I'll bring ya a tray. We'll be in the kitchen. Ya need anything else, call out."

We sat near the woodstove, Cordie rising from time to time to stir the soup and check on the cornbread as I lifted the grate to add more wood to the stove. She went to the cupboard, took down a tin of black pepper and dusted the top of the soup, then ladled up enough to taste. She pursed her lips and sighed.

"Oh, how I miss having a little deer meat for soup. Just can't hardly get any flavor without it. I hope this pepper will help it along." She sat down staring at the pot of soup.

"Larraine, see what I mean about Otha saying strange things. Talking about that old hound being an angel and taking him to heaven. Do ya think he's making up stories in his head? He always could take anything and make up a story about it."

"No, Cordie. I think he really believes Pity is his angel."

We sat silent 'til the soup was done and the heat of the woodstove began to fade. Cordie took down a worn wooden tray from a nail along the wall. She cut a big piece of cornbread, filled a bowl with the soup, poured the last of the buttermilk into a mug and placed it all on the tray. She picked up the tray and smiled.

"This tray is one of the treasures Otha brought home when he was working as the night watchman at the dump. He spent all afternoon sanding it smooth and rubbing it with linseed oil so I wouldn't get no splinters in my hands. I'm gonna take his supper to him now."

Then came the howl. The long, loud doleful cry sounded throughout the farmhouse, echoing off the walls. Cordie dropped the tray. The bowl and mug shattered, spraying shards of glass, soup and buttermilk on her legs and feet. She uttered quietly, "He's gone."

We sat at Otha's bedside. Cordie with her head down softly sobbing. Pity continued to howl. He wailed mournfully as if in pain and sorrow. Cordie rose from her chair, wiped away her tears with her apron, went to the window, pulled back the curtain and looked out.

"The snow has stopped. It left with Otha. Otha loved and held to these forty acres of earth as a mother would hold to her child. I hope it wasn't too hard for him to leave this piece of earth that he tended for so many years. I never once said to him that I loved him, but I did love him. After the river took my first husband it just wasn't my way to say I love ya to anybody. Go to the kitchen, Larraine, and fix a bowl of soup and cornbread for old Pity. Maybe that'll ease him a little."

I brought the bowl to Pity but he had no interest. He threw back his head and filled the room with more howls. I sat down on the floor next to him holding the bowl up to his nose, patting his head 'til he took a few small bites, laid down on the quilt and fell asleep. Cordie stayed at the window staring out at the white fields.

"Larraine, there're things to be done. Put more wood on the fires and put a kettle of water on the woodstove to heat. I need to bathe Otha. Then ya bundle up real good. Ya will have to walk the three miles to Mr. Fields store. He sold his house and lives in the back of the store now. He's a little hard a hearing so just keep banging on the door 'til he hears ya. Tell him Otha has passed. He'll know who to call and what to do. Get going. Be safe."

I walked the white landscape mirrored above by a fading white sky. There was such a quiet stillness about the earth and sky that night. The earth beneath my feet gave up no landmarks but I knew the way. The sky above quickly faded from light to dark but I could see. I was numb but not from the cold. From the moment Pity began to howl something had shut down inside me. I had not yet cried or knew if I could because none of it seemed real. But, Otha knew. He had known from the day that Pity came to him. Otha knew he was leaving and he had tried in his own way to tell me and Cordie.

Throughout my childhood Otha had taught me that everything had a reason, a natural way of being. He believed that every person, plant and animal on earth held and possessed beauty and magic in its own way. With Otha, there was always magic to be found and stories to be told. I realized that night while walking through the snow to beckon Mr. Fields that Otha and Pity had given me the greatest story of all. And in that thought a rush of comfort filled me and the numbness left. I ran through the snow, laughing, making snowballs and pelting the pines along the way.

I don't remember arriving at Mr. Fields door or any conversation with him. There was a void, empty space of memory filled with only cold and darkness. Next came a flood of movements, voices, sounds and scents and hands.

Mr. Fields lifting me from the cab of his truck, carrying me up the porch steps through the farmhouse and placing me in a rocker next to the fireplace. Then his voice, low and muffled as if he were in a tunnel.

"When I opened my door, she was standing there smiling with an armload of snowballs. All she said before she collapsed was, Cordie wants you to come quick, we need a back-stick and then something about Pity taking Otha. Who is Pity? What's happened, Cordie?"

"Pity is that old hound sitting over there next to the rocker with Larraine. Otha has passed. I sent Larraine to fetch ya."

"I'm so sorry, Cordie. I'll go back home and call the undertaker and your preacher, then round up some of the neighbors. The roads are still really bad so it might take us a while to get back here. Will you be all right? Is Larraine all right?"

"Larraine takes and handles things different than most folks. We'll both be all right. Thank ya."

Silence. Movements. The sound of a door closing. Cordie taking off my boots, hat and gloves. Her hands on mine rubbing them briskly, taking away the cold. Putting a quilt about my shoulders. Pity's warm, moist nose nudging my hand. The sound of the fire poker shifting wood. More warmth. Cordie reading aloud. "Yea, though I walk through the valley of the shadow of death, I will fear no evil. For thou art with me..."

The sound of knocking. More voices. The room alive with movement. The smell of fried chicken, baked apples, salt pork and turnip greens. Hands on my shoulder and hugs around my neck. More knocking, more people. They came throughout the night, moving all the chairs in the farmhouse next to the fireplace. Prayers, song, the scent of food and the sound of forks striking plates, and voices in low tones in between.

"Roads are still bad. The undertaker can't get here 'til morning..."
"You and the girl all alone now..."
"Yes, Cordie, you should get a telephone. Case of emergencies..."
"Otha was a good, hardworking man..."
"The church will help with the burial..."
"Honey, you want a piece of chicken or maybe a bowl of greens..."
"Cordie, the girl don't look well..."
Silence.

"Larraine. Larraine. Larraine, ya need to wake up."

Cordie was at my bedside. Pity stood next to her, his tail wagging.

"Ya got to get up out of this bed. Otha will be taking to the ground tomorrow."

"Is Otha here?"

"No. The undertaker came for him two days ago. Ya been stone cold out since the night of his passing. Had me really worried. I was afraid I'd lose ya too. After they took Otha Pity come in here and lay next to your bed. So I put his quilt on the floor and he's been waiting for ya to wake up."

"Oh, Cordie. I am so sorry. I don't know what happened to me. I should have been helping you, keeping the fires stoked and making arrangements for the funeral."

"Men from my church been coming ever day to keep the fires going. It ain't as cold as afore. Had a little sunshine, so most of the snow has melted and the ground thawed enough for digging Otha's grave. All the arrangements been made. The service will be tomorrow at two."

"But, Cordie, I don't own a dress."

Cordie laughed and patted my shoulder. "Don't fret about that. Otha loved and knew ya just the way ya are. Wear ya jeans. If ya showed up to his taking to the ground in a dress I can see Otha looking down and wondering who that strange girl sitting next to me is."

We passed the day gathering eggs, doing the milking and laying out our clothes for the service. Pity followed close at my heels, sometimes bumping into the back of my legs.

"Well, Larraine, looks like with Otha gone that old hound done took up with ya. He never did have no use for me, even though I was the one that fed him ever day. Seems like he just needs a cause and now he's picked ya as his cause."

"I don't mind, Cordie. In a way Pity makes me feel like Otha is still here with us. I hope that doesn't sound like crazy talk."

"No, it don't sound crazy at all."

When night came we sat by the fire and talked about the next day. Cordie told me that she had asked Mr. Fields to call Ruby and let her know about Otha's passing. She said Mr. Fields made the call but Ruby said she was ill again and could not come.

"Cordie, in one of your letters you said Mama was divorcing Daddy. Did she?"

"No. My, that's been about a year ago since Ruby said that to me. She used to come by once in a while. When I sent ya that letter she was talking about it. Haven't seen or talked to Ruby since. Now wait, she did come by one more time and said she was sick with the headaches again. She didn't speak no more about divorcing George. They still together."

"So, Mama and Daddy don't know I'm here?"

"Not to my knowing. If they did I'm sure they would have showed up by now. It's getting late but if ya don't mind put a little more wood on the fire. I ain't quite ready for bed yet."

"How about Little Brother? Do you ever get news from him?"

"He wrote me one letter when he got out west. I wrote a letter to him but my letter come back saying he was not at that address no more. Never heard another word from him. Wish I knew he was okay."

I built up the fire and stayed with Cordie. Both of us sitting in silence with Otha's empty rocker between us. Occasionally Cordie would look over at it and smile.

"Cordie, you want me to take Otha's rocker to another room?"

"Heavens, no! Remember what ya said earlier today about feeling like Otha is still here with us? Ain't nothing crazy about feeling that way. I do too. Matter a fact I know he's close by cause he came to me last night."

"You had a dream about him?"

"No, Larraine, it weren't no dream. From time to time last night ya called out in your sleep. I stayed up, sitting in my rocker near the fire, hoping ya would wake up and I could fix ya something to eat. Long about eleven o'clock Pity left your bedside and come in here. He went right over to Otha's rocker, looked up at it, then laid down next to it. The fire had nearly burnt down to nothing but suddenly the coals were gold again and the room got warmer. That's when I heard him call my name. I looked back at his rocker and he was there smiling at me."

"But, Cordie. It had to be a dream."

"Do ya remember the story I told ya about the red-haired lady at the sulfur springs and how I believe that the dead do come back. How sometimes they just want ya to know they're okay. Sometimes they come to say they love ya and sometimes they come to ask something of ya."

"I do remember the story. When I went back home that summer I looked for a sign from Ionia. But never saw anything."

"Well, maybe your grandmother Ionia ain't ready to contact ya yet. I bet in your lifetime ya will see her or a sign from her."

"What did Otha say to you?"

"Well after he called my name, he sat there tapping his foot on the floor, reached down and patted Pity's head, smiled, then held his hands out to the heat coming from the fireplace. He told me his legs didn't give him no trouble anymore and he felt as fit as the day we married. He said I should wake ya up come morning and me and ya go on about the business of burying him and then back to the business of living. He said he loved us and made me promise to take care of and not let any harm come to ya and Pity. I told him long as there was a breath in me, I would. Then with one more smile, he faded away."

"Do you think you'll see him again?"

"Don't know. But I do believe he'll always be close by. Best we both get to bed. Tomorrow gone be a long day."

We were up at sunrise. Cordie made strong coffee, biscuits and mixed up a bowl of butter and molasses to spread on the hot biscuits. We went about the morning chores of feeding the farm animals, gathering eggs and milking Li'l Belle. Then we cleaned every room of the farmhouse. Cordie said the neighbors would be bringing food after the service. She covered the kitchen table with a checkered tablecloth and set out plates and silverware. At noon we ate the leftover breakfast biscuits, butter and molasses, then we bathed and dressed and waited for Mr. Fields to arrive to take us to the church.

For a man who had never entered a church door, Otha was well respected in the community. Every pew in the little one room church was filled, the men giving up their seats to the women, then standing along the walls and at the back of the church. The preacher's eulogy was brief and the casket closed as Otha wanted. I looked about the room, fearful that James Lee might be in attendance but did not see him. Otha was carried from the church to his resting place in the cemetery. Cordie and I followed first, then his friends, members of the church and his neighbors.

We sat at the graveside, Cordie holding my hand as the preacher said last words and prayers. As he spoke Cordie squeezed my hand and leaned toward me, whispering in my ear. "George is here."

"Where?"

"Across the way."

I looked at the group of men on the other side of the grave but didn't see Daddy.

"Cordie. I don't see him."

"Larraine, ya probably wouldn't recognize him now. He's standing two rows in among the men, wearing a tan leisure suit, blue shirt and red tie. Don't worry. He ain't gonna take ya anywhere."

I looked again and it was Daddy. His face thin and hollow, his eyes with no look of life in them. He stood, his face red, staring directly at me and Cordie. I wanted to run but Cordie held fast to my hand. Mr. Fields had seen Daddy in the crowd too. When the burial was finished he came to me and Cordie, placed his hands at the small of our backs, escorting us across the cemetery. Within a few yards Daddy's hand was on my shoulder pulling me back and around to face him. His breath was heavy with whiskey, his voice deep.

"When the hell did you get back?"

Mr. Fields grabbed Daddy's hand and stepped in between us. Cordie tried to push past Mr. Fields. She was yelling, "Leave her alone, George! Leave her alone!"

Daddy tried to break free of Mr. Fields grip on his hand. When Mr. Fields let him go Daddy stumbled backwards, regained his footing and began shouting. "Don't ever put your goddamn hands on me again, Fields!" The mourners leaving the cemetery heard him and they came back forming a circle around us. Daddy looked at them and shouted louder.

"This is none of your goddamn business. Go on home to your cornbread and peas. It's none of Fields' business either! Or Cordie's business! Larraine's my kid and she needs to come home and take care of her mama. Cause I damn sure don't know what to do with Ruby. Cordie, you remember Ruby, don't you? Ruby! Ruby! You know, that crazy bitch daughter of yours that hooked me into marrying her. Larraine's going home with me to take care of crazy Ruby!"

Daddy took a few steps toward us. Mr. Fields held his position between Daddy and me and Cordie. The crowd of mourners pushed closer.

"George, this ain't the time or the place for this. Your daughter is where she wants to be. You need to go on home and sober up."

"Shut the hell up, Fields! Get out of my way!"

Eight men, long time neighbors of Cordie and Otha, left the circle of mourners and stood next to Mr. Fields forming a wall. Mr. Fields pointed his finger at Daddy and this time when he spoke his voice was louder so that all who were around us could hear.

"George, this is over. You're gonna leave this cemetery now. And, don't you ever again darken the door of my store. Your money ain't no good to me. And, you see all these people around you? We know you and what your truck looks like. Any of us see you in our neighborhood we're gonna call the law and tell 'em you're driving drunk. Now go!"

There was a moment of silence. Daddy lit a cigarette, took a deep draw from it and then flicked it at Mr. Fields chest. Without a word, the mourners formed two lines shoulder to shoulder leading out to the road and Daddy's truck. Mr. Fields shouted again.

"I said, it's time for you to go, George!"

Daddy looked at the mourners and the path they'd made. He lit another cigarette and pointed down the line of men and women.

"My mother was right! I should have listened to her and never hooked up with Ruby. Ruby was born to hillbillies and all the rest of you are hillbillies. Bible-thumping backward hillbillies! And all you men standing here? You think I don't know that while your wives are cooking Sunday dinner for the preacher, you're sneaking off to the barn for a nip of homemade shine? Hypocrites! Every goddamn one of you are hypocrites!"

Daddy turned back to Mr. Fields, me and Cordie. He walked closer, pointing his finger inches from Mr. Fields face.

"Fields, you and none of the rest of these ignorant hillbillies can stop me from going where I want to go. If I decide to go to Cordie's and drag this sorry daughter of mine back home with me, there's nothing none of you can do. And you know what else Fields? I know what your truck looks like. If I was you, I wouldn't be out on these country roads after dark."

No one spoke. Everyone held their position, all eyes on Daddy. He looked once more at the mourners.

"Hell, you're not worth my time."

He stumbled down the center of the path they'd made, cursing and spitting on the shoes of both men and women along the line. When he reached his truck he revved the engine, put the truck in gear and drove over a section of older grave markers along the roadway.

Cordie put her arms around me. "It's okay. He'll never take ya from the farm. I promise. It's over and we'll never speak of it again. Let's go home."

We didn't speak of it again, nor did any of the neighbors who came to the farm that afternoon bringing food. They talked about the coming of spring and the crops they planned to put in the ground. And their hope for good weather and to not be plagued by too many snakes come summer. That was the way of country folk. They survived the bad and put it aside. Their talk, glances in my direction and smiles were an unspoken comfort and reassurance that they would be watching for Daddy.

Jan Fink

SEVENTEEN

Throughout the remaining days of winter, Cordie and I made plans for our spring garden. We decided to break a small patch of ground next to the vegetable plot and add a strawberry patch. Men from the church continued to cut wood for us and bring it to the farm. We missed Otha so much, as did Pity. He would lie next to Otha's rocker each evening as we sat by the fireside. Sometimes during the night he would leave his quilt on the floor next to my bed and I'd find him sitting, staring up at the empty rocker. I wondered if Otha came back to us often and Pity could sense his presence when Cordie and I couldn't.

Pity's age seemed to bother him more. There were days when his lame leg didn't want to serve him at all. He slept a lot, sometimes dreaming and yelping, his legs running in place as if he were young again and on the hunt. Good days or bad he remained protective of me and Cordie. At the slightest sound of a whippoorwill calling or the cry of a coyote from the woodland, he was on his feet running to the front or back door wanting out to find the intruder. Those nights he slept on the porch, yelping from time to time at things in the dark. Come sunrise, he was clawing at the door to come back in.

It was the first warm summer night of that new year that we were awakened by Pity howling and clawing the front door, wanting out. Then the sound of a horn blowing in front of the house. Cordie was already at the window next to the front door. She whispered, "Stay quiet. Don't let Pity out. It's James Lee."

She moved away from the window and locked the front door. The sound of the truck horn stopped, then the headlights began blinking off and on from dim to bright. Bright to dim, then darkness.

"Larraine, let's play a game! Larraine, Larraine, come out, come out wherever you are!"

Cordie put her finger to her lips and whispered, "Go out the back door into the high brush of the field, lie down and hide 'til he leaves."

"No, Cordie. I will not leave you here alone."

The horn began to blow again, this time the headlights blinking along with it. Then silence followed by James Lee calling out.

"I know you're in there little girl! Come on out, Larraine! All I want to do is go for a ride and just play a game with you!"

James Lee had said the same words to me that day in the woodland about Johnny. That he was just playing a game with him. An over whelming anger rushed me. I went down on my hands and knees and crawled to Otha's room and his gun rack. I took down the shotgun, loaded it and went back to Cordie. When she saw the gun her eyes went wide.

"Larraine! Is that shotgun loaded?" I whispered yes.

"Ya give it to me right now."

"No, Cordie. James Lee is dangerous. He'll kill us."

Cordie took the shotgun from me and removed the shells, put them in the pocket of her housecoat, then took my hand.

"James Lee is drunk but he ain't gone kill nobody. And we ain't gone kill him. I'm gonna open the door a crack. Ya hold onto to Pity and don't let him run out."

Still holding the shotgun Cordie opened the door and yelled out, "James Lee!"

"Yes ma'am, Miss Cordie, it's me, James Lee. Tell Larraine to come on out and play."

"James Lee, Otha done told ya not to come round here no more. I think ya had too much to drink tonight. Best ya go on home."

"Ah, but Otha ain't here no more is he, Miss Cordie? Send Larraine out to play or I'll have to come in and get her."

Cordie opened the door and stepped out on the porch still holding the shotgun. James Lee was sitting on the hood of his truck.

"Now ya listen to me real good, James Lee. Larraine ain't coming out. She's on the phone right now calling the law. Best ya be on your way."

"You ain't and never have had a damn phone, Miss Cordie."

James Lee slid down off the hood of his truck and started toward the farmhouse. Cordie raised the shotgun, pointing it in his direction.

"Ya don't really know, now do ya, James Lee? Maybe I have a phone or maybe I don't. But as ya can see I got this here shotgun in my hands. Ya still really want to play with Larraine?"

James Lee held up his hands and backed away toward his truck laughing and smiling. Cordie stayed on the porch, shotgun raised 'til he was down the lane, onto the main road and the sound of his truck no more. She came back inside, returned Otha's gun to the gun rack, then went to her rocker and sat silent.

"Cordie, he'll be back. I know he will. He'll come back and next time he'll bring the boys with him."

Cordie sighed. "Are ya talking about the boys that used to ride over here with him?"

"Yes. They'll do anything James Lee tells them to. He'll bring the boys and next time an empty shotgun won't stop him."

"Larraine, ya don't have to worry about that happening. Ain't a one of 'em boys still living."

"What do you mean?"

"I'm telling ya that ever one of 'em is dead. One drank 'til his liver give out. A tractor rolled on one and crushed him. And the last one run his car off the road at Turkey Creek Hill and smashed into the bluffs. Ya and James Lee are the only ones left from the days of your riding club."

"But Cordie, James Lee will still come back."

"Larraine, I know growing up in George and Ruby's house ya seen things a child ought not to see. And I know 'em things scared ya, but ya can't be scared all ya life. James Lee ain't no different than a lot of boys and men who take to drinking beer, whiskey or homemade shine. The drink makes 'em feel powerful like they can do anything but in most cases when the drink wears off so does that feeling of power. Come morning, I bet James Lee will feel real bad about coming over here. Quit worrying. Let's get back to bed."

I spent a sleepless night, the slightest sound was magnified. More than anything I wanted to wake Cordie and tell her why I was scared. How dangerous I knew James Lee was, but I couldn't. To tell her meant exposing all my lies.

EIGHTEEN

The summer passed quickly. From our small garden Cordie and I picked and canned jar after jar of vegetables 'til the larder was filled. Even our strawberry patch yielded enough fruit for two dozen jars of preserves. Cordie was especially proud of the preserves. Each time she went to the larder she'd touch the jars, smile and say what a sweet treasure they would be on a warm, buttered biscuit come a cold winter day.

Once a month Mr. Fields would drive us to the cemetery to visit Otha's grave. Sometimes we'd pick wildflowers and lay them on his resting place. On other visits Cordie would stand at his graveside and talk to him. She told him of the weather, the garden and all the vegetables we'd put up during the summer. And most important, the strawberry patch we'd added and how she wished he could see what beautiful preserves the fruit had made. On each visit she also told him that his old hound, Pity, was still alive and well and doing a good job protecting me and her.

For the first month after the night James Lee came to the farm I was never at ease. I asked Cordie to have a phone installed but she refused, saying she didn't see the need or expense of having a phone. Throughout the summer James Lee never came back. The work on the farm kept my mind busy and with time I began to think that maybe Cordie was right. It was simply the drink that made James Lee brave that night. I hoped it was and that he had tired of trying to make sure I had kept silent his transgression.

When the nights brought a chill, the men from the church came with wood for the coming of winter. They arrived with twice as much wood and kindling as the winter before in case of another heavy snow and ice storm. Neighbors also brought us bags of field corn for Li'l Belle and the chickens. When it became too cold for visits with neighbors on the front porch Cordie brought out her quilting frame and invited the neighbor women over once a week. They sat next to the fire bent over the quilting frame, talking as their fingers worked feverishly, making tiny stitches across the fabric.

I knew Cordie still missed Otha but those days with her friends at the quilting frame, working, talking and sharing recipes made her so happy. With Cordie there was always a project or work of some kind to keep her hands and mind busy. It was her coping skill in good times and bad. I envied her because in my case no amount of work or talk erased the thought of James Lee's eventual return to the farm.

Unlike the winter before, the weather this winter was a wild ride of warm, sunny days, then days of bitter cold and freezing rain. The anniversary of Otha's passing was drawing near and the temperature had dropped to thirty-five degrees by nightfall. As we sat by the fire, I asked Cordie if she thought snow would come again.

She smiled and patted Pity's head. "No. Don't believe we'll get snow. I think the snow came last winter for Otha, just like this old angel hound came to take him to heaven."

"Otha really did love that snow, didn't he, Cordie?"

"He truly did. Specially throwing 'em snowballs at ya. And he loved this old hound here too." Pity looked up at Cordie and licked her ankle.

"Well, I'll be! Did ya see that, Larraine? All this time Pity ain't never give me a glance. Now he's wanting to friend me up. We gotta mark this date down. The day Pity give me his blessing!" We both laughed. Pity got up and began to yelp and we laughed harder. He continued to yelp and began pacing between me and Cordie.

"Larraine, we either got Pity so excited he needs to go outside and pee or he hears something in the woods. Best ya let him out."

I opened the front door and Pity left the porch, his nose to the ground, tracking and making his way around the side of the house toward the back field. I went back to the fireside and sat with Cordie.

"Cordie, Pity was tracking something across the yard and back towards the field behind the house. You think I should call him back in?"

"Wouldn't do ya no good to call him. He might have picked up the scent of a fox wandering round the yard after my chickens. He'll come back by morning, like always, scratching on the door to be let in."

Several times early in the night I heard Pity's yelps. He was still on the hunt. When I woke in the morning Cordie was in the kitchen and had already built a fire in the cookstove. A pot of coffee was simmering, her hands were covered with flour and she was rolling out biscuits and placing them in a big iron skillet. She looked up and smiled.

"Morning."

"Morning, Cordie. You're up early and busy. Did you let Pity in?"

"Sun's out and already burned off the morning frost. Ain't much dampness in the air today so I got up feeling full of vigor. And no, I ain't heard Pity at the door this morning. He's probably still chasing that fox. I wouldn't eat a fox but I sure wouldn't mind if he caught a squirrel while he was hunting one night and brought it home to us. I would love to have fried squirrel, gravy and biscuits for breakfast."

"He should have been back by morning. He always is, Cordie. I'll go call him."

"Afore ya do, go draw me an extra bucket of water. Can't have squirrel for breakfast but I think I'll do something different this morning and boil us some eggs. We can mash 'em with a pat of butter and a little pepper and salt and they'll be good with our biscuits and coffee."

Cordie took the iron skillet of biscuits and put it in the oven of the cookstove. She picked up a small piece of firewood, lifted the cookstove grate and dropped it in. Then she went to the kitchen counter, sank her hands into a dishpan of water, washing away the flour and dough that clung to her fingers. She began to hum.

I went outside and stood on the back porch looking out over the fields, hoping to see Pity. From the kitchen I could hear Cordie's voice, now in song.

Shall we gather at the river
Where bright angel feet have trod,

With its crystal tide forever
Flowing by the throne of God?

"Larraine! Hurry up with that water! I need to get the eggs boiled afore the biscuits get done!"

I went down the steps to the well and pushed back the heavy steel plate that covered it. I unhooked the chain and bucket from the nail on the well post and let the bucket fall from the pulley into the well. Hand over hand I attempted to pull the bucket up but it was heavy, barely rising more than a couple of feet. I held the chain steady, stood on my tiptoes and looked down into the well. The water was blood red and the bucket was cradling Pity's head.

Stumbling backward I let go of the chain. It ran its length through the pulley, loudly rattling off the links in the chain one by one. I went down on my knees and tried to call out to Cordie but the only thing that came from my mouth was the sound of dry-heaving. Everything fell silent, no bird calls from the woodland or the clucking of the yard chickens. There was nothing but the sound of Cordie's voice.

Yes, we'll gather at the river,
The beautiful, the beautiful river;
Gather with the saints at the river
That flows by the throne of God…

"Larraine! Did ya fall?"

Cordie was kneeling next to me, her hand on my shoulder. I pointed in the direction of the well.

"Pity."

Cordie stood and looked across the yard and out at the back field.

"Where Larraine? I don't see him." Cordie knelt next to me again and pulled my face toward hers. "Larraine, what's wrong. Where's Pity?"

"He's...he's in the well, Cordie. He's in the well!"

"That can't be. We always keep the well covered."

I began to sob and pointed toward the well again. Cordie walked slowly to the well and looked down into it. She cried out, then pulled her apron up to her face, covering her eyes and backed away quickly. Suddenly she let her apron fall and she looked down at the ground around the well.

"Somebody's been here during the night. Get inside now, Larraine!"

Cordie walked quickly to me, grabbed my arm and pushed me toward the back door. I didn't have to look back. I knew what Cordie saw on the ground. She saw footprints. James

Lee's footprints. And I knew it was time to confess all my past secret lies to her and Otha.

In the kitchen we sat at the table, smoke and the smell of burning biscuits from the cookstove oven filled the room. "Cordie, the biscuits are burning." She sat dazed, looking at the back door. "Cordie?"

It was a moment before she got up without saying a word and pulled the biscuits from the oven. She stood looking down at them, then went to the cupboard, brought back a butter knife and attempted to scrape the charcoaled tops off the biscuits. The more she tried the more the biscuits crumbled. Then she turned, looked at me and began to cry.

"I promised Otha that I'd take care of ya and old Pity. It looks like I ain't done a good job of it."

"Don't cry, Cordie. You know Pity didn't fall in the well. It was James Lee who put him there. I told you he'd come back."

"Larraine, I just can't take it to my heart that James Lee would do such a thing. I know his mama and daddy and they're good folks. James Lee been coming here to the farm since he was a little kid."

"There's something I have to tell you, Cordie. It's about the riding club, James Lee, the boys, me and Johnny."

I told Cordie everything from the beginning to that last day. The day we all rode into the woodland and what happened at the Duck John place. Tears began to fall down her cheeks. She reached out and took my hand in hers and squeezed it tightly.

"Oh, Lord, Larraine! All this time, Johnny's mama taking care of her boy, burying him and not knowing what happened that day in the woodland cause Johnny couldn't tell her. None of us knowing what really happened that day. Why didn't ya tell somebody? Why didn't ya tell me and Otha?"

"Because I was afraid of James Lee. I've been even more afraid since that first day he showed up here after I came back to live with you and Otha. Now that the boys are all dead I'm the only witness, the only one who knows what really happened to Johnny. I'm so sorry that I didn't speak up and that I lied to you and Otha, but now you know what James Lee is capable of. He will not stop 'til he ends me. He'll be back."

"Otha must have sensed your fear that day when James Lee came asking ya all 'em questions. That must be why he put him on the road and told him not to come back here. Otha made me promise to look after ya, Larraine, and now I don't know how. What can we do? If we tell Mr. Fields what James Lee did to Johnny and that he was now giving ya trouble, he could report it to the law and have the neighbors watch out for us 'til the law catches James Lee and locks him up."

"No, Cordie! We're not going to tell Mr. Fields or anybody else anything. Not about Johnny or James Lee coming to the farm or finding Pity in the well."

"We have to tell somebody. We need help, Larraine. We don't have Otha to protect us or old Pity to warn us if James Lee comes back in the night. We can't get Pity out of the well by ourselves. The well water is spoilt. What we gone do for water?"

"Cordie, please promise me you won't tell anyone. Even if they locked James Lee up, it wouldn't be forever. I'll do anything. I can bring up jugs of water from the little creek in the back field and we can get by with that. And don't you worry about protecting me. It's my time to protect you."

I went to Otha's room, took down his shotgun and loaded it, then to the back porch where Otha kept a coil of rope. I cut enough length from the coil to make a shoulder strap, tying one end to the barrel and the other to the stock. When I re-entered the kitchen Cordie was still at the table. She looked up, her eyes red from crying. The sight of the gun brought more tears.

"No, Larraine. Put that away. This ain't the right way. From the time ya was a little girl me and Otha worried about ya. We knowed what ya had been through and feared that it would turn your heart yellah and poisonous like the bitterweed. We tried to love all the hurt out of ya by showing and teaching ya the good. In spite of all that me and Otha did for ya, is that what's happening to ya now? Has your heart finally turned yellah and poisonous?"

"No, Cordie. I think my heart has always been poisonous."

The shotgun never left my shoulder, not even in sleep. The slightest sound during the dark hours woke me. I'd leave my bed and go to the windows, pressing my ear to the cold glass panes, straining to hear and identify the sound. Those nights as I lay awake I began to slowly recall a lesson Otha had taught me. He had described to me the sounds of things unseen in the night.

The sound of the soft paws of coyotes, bobcats and foxes on the hunt. The sound of possums scratching in the dry leaves of fall and winter looking for grubs. And the sound of a heavier predator, man.

I stayed in Otha's room when Cordie and her friends met to quilt. When Mr. Fields came to take us to visit Otha's grave,

Cordie declined. I heard her on the porch telling him that she wasn't feeling well, maybe another time.

Cordie had been quiet since seeing Pity in the well. Even as we sat at the fireside in the evenings she had little to say to me other than she could not go to the cemetery and talk to Otha. She said she could not bring herself to tell him of all that had happened since he left.

The anniversary of Otha's death came and went as did the months of winter and Cordie still refused to visit his graveside. She took down the quilting frame, stopped inviting her friends over and spent her time reading the Bible and praying. She rarely looked in my direction and I knew why. The shotgun on my shoulder was a glimpse of things to come that she didn't want to see or embrace. It was sad but for me the comfort of the gun was necessary.

NINETEEN

With spring came heavy rain. It was in the muck and mud of six days of downpour while milking Li'l Belle that I heard him approach. I waited and listened to the rain hitting the tin roof of the lean-to and the sound of his boots. With each step his boots made an air-sucking sound as he pulled them free of the mud. I counted the sound of his footsteps one by one 'til I knew he was a few yards away. Only then did I rise from the milking stool and turn to him. He stood there outside smiling and pulled one boot free of the mud, his arms outstretched, balancing himself like a tightrope walker.

"Hey, Larraine. Look what you made me do. Made me ruin my best shirt and good pair of boots trying to sneak up on you. I just want to ask you some questions. You know what I'm talking about, girl? That little queer, Johnny Redboots?"

He took off his shirt, held it up, attempted to wring the rainwater from it then laughed and threw it in the mud near the lean-to. I stood quiet with one hand on the rope strap of the shotgun and the other hand resting on Li'l Belle's back. Li'l Belle moved from side to side, restless and wanting free of the lean-to.

"You still don't understand that I was protecting you that day. I told you then that Johnny Redboots would have never been your boyfriend. Me on the other hand, well, I would have loved and protected you forever. But then you up and disappeared and that worried me. It's been a while, but I need to know. If you'd just told me the first time I came back here to the farm that you'd not told anybody what happened that day, I'd left you alone, but I don't know yet who you've talked to.

You shouldn't have run off. Put yourself in my place. How do I know you ain't told somebody? That's what worries me the most. I've been sitting around all this time waiting for the law to show up at my door. So tell me now if you told anybody."

"We know you put Pity in the well. Go away, James Lee, and leave us alone."

"Pity? That's what you called him? Perfect, because he was pitiful. That old hound didn't have no more fight in him than Otha had with his two bum legs."

James Lee laughed and clapped his hands. Li'l Belle lowered her head and her movements became more frantic. The bell on her collar ringing loudly within the small lean-to. It was as if she sensed the tension between me and James Lee. She tried backing out of the lean-to. I caught her collar and rubbed my hand along her cheek but it did little to calm her. James Lee stopped laughing and watched as I tried to soothe her, one moment his face was somber then the next moment he was smiling.

"Ah, Larraine, did you tell Miss Cordie?"

"Go away, James Lee! Don't come back here again!"

"I do believe you did tell her. Now ain't that a shame. I didn't have no quarrel with Miss Cordie as long as you didn't tell her. But now you've gone and pulled her into it. Yep, what a shame. But she'll probably go down as easy as that old hound did."

He took one step closer, the air-sucking sound of his boots now magnified. I pulled the shotgun forward and pointed it in his direction. He looked at the gun and stopped and stood laughing, his mouth wide open. He was now close enough that I could smell the whiskey on his breath.

"Larraine, Larraine, Larraine. All this over a little queer with a big mouth. If you'd just stayed by the pond that day like I told you none of this would be necessary. You can stand there and point that empty gun at me but here's how it's all gonna play out. Miss Cordie is gonna take her last nap with the help of a pillow over her face. She's old, people will think she died in her sleep. And you, Larraine? That cow you're milking seems to me to be a real nervous animal. When I get through with you, people are gonna think that cow got spooked and you got trampled. The whole community will shake their heads and say how sad, poor old Miss Cordie and her granddaughter went to their maker on the same day."

He leaned forward suddenly and raised his hands above his head. The corners of his mouth twisted downward and he yelled. "Boo!" Li'l Belle bolted from the lean-to and I pulled the trigger. An ear shattering thunderous boom echoed across the pasture. The bone chilling blast of the shotgun was the final sound of freedom.

James Lee's face did not register any emotion nor did he make a sound. Small blood filled craters and torn flesh covered his chest. Below his heart the raw bone of his ribcage was exposed. The sky opened up, dropping more rain. For a brief moment he stood there, his eyes open and staring, the rain carrying his blood down the front of his chest and onto his jeans. Then he went down, short of me, like an ill thrown rock. He fell backwards, the mud and muck holding his boots in place, leaving his knees bent upward as if he were simply lying on his back looking up at the sun on a beautiful day. There was no sun. The storm clouds hovered above, the sky dark, the rain heavier, puddling around James Lee.

I looked up at the dark sky, letting the rain fall on my face. When I looked down Cordie was there on her knees beside James Lee. Her mouth was moving in what I knew was prayer but I couldn't hear her words. I watched as the muddy, bloody rainwater soaked the white of her apron, turning it dirty brick red, the color seeping upwards toward her waist.

"Get up, Cordie! He's not worth your prayers!"

She looked up at me, an expression on her face that all those years with her, I had never seen before.

"I ain't praying for James Lee. I'm praying for ya, Larraine." She lowered her head again, her mouth once more moving in silent prayer. Minutes passed before she pulled herself from the mud and stood facing me.

"Go get Mr. Fields."

"No, Cordie. Like Pity, no one will ever know about this. James Lee came here today to kill both of us."

"Then ya was defending us. The law won't lock ya up for that."

"I don't know what the law will or won't do. I only know what has to be done. James Lee is going back to the woodland where it all started. We'll bury him next to the pond under the devil's snuff at Duck John's home place. The ground is soft there. The timber company still owns the land. It'll be another ten to twenty years, maybe more before they clear cut and re-plant. There won't be much left of James Lee by then."

"But, Larraine, this ain't right."

"Yes it is, Cordie. It's right and it's just. Go to the house and bring all the rope from the back porch and a shovel."

I watched as Cordie made her way to the farmhouse and then back to the lean-to. She moved slowly, the rope in one hand, the other hand dragging the shovel behind her, her head down, mouth still moving in prayer. I loved her so dearly and for a moment I thought my heart would splinter but I knew I had done what had to be done.

Cordie dropped the rope and shovel in the mud and stood watching as I took the rope and tied James Lee's shirt over his head and the shotgun across his chest. Then I fashioned a harness under his arms and upper body with enough rope to loop over my shoulders to pull him. I picked up the shovel and put it in Cordie's hand.

"Cordie, you have to help me. You have to carry the shovel. I can't drag him and hold the shovel too." She took the shovel and stood silent, still looking down at James Lee.

With the first pull his boots left his feet. They stood there upright in the mud, rain puddling inside them. I pulled them free, took the last piece of rope and tied them to the shotgun across his chest. Once free of the mud in the lean-to lot the rain-slicked grass of the pasture made pulling James Lee's weight easier. Li'l Belle stood in the middle of the pasture watching our progress with wide-eyed curiosity.

When we reached the woodland it was slow going. Every few yards it was necessary to stop and clear downed limbs and brush from the path. We reached Duck John's Place by noon, under an overcast sky, the rain still falling. The devil's snuff lay in wet soggy clumps around the pond and the chimney was still there, standing like the statues of Easter Island, once more a witness and testament to time and secrets.

I thought of Johnny and our picnic next to the pond and of our childhood innocence. For a moment I wanted Johnny and Velvet back. But Velvet wasn't coming back, nor was Johnny and our childhood innocence was long lost. I knew even in James Lee's death peace would be hard to find.

It took 'til dusk to dig the hole deep enough, shoveling through wet layers of soil filled with fat, wiggly earthworms, rotted wood, nails, stones and old rusty tin cans from Duck John's larder. The rain fell heavier and thunder echoed in the woodland as I rolled James Lee into the hole. He landed face down. Appropriate, I thought, now he would see nothing but hell. As I tossed the first shovel of soil onto his back I whispered into the rain.

"It's over, Johnny. James Lee will never hurt anyone again. Rest in peace. It's all over."

Cordie sat at the base of a large pine as I filled in the hole. She was soaked by the rain and still praying. I went to help her up but she refused to take my hand, holding to the trunk of the pine and pulling herself up. When she was on her feet she turned to me and in a stern voice said.

"I heard what ya said. It ain't over. Ya think putting James Lee in that hole is gonna end everything and make it better and over? It ain't never gonna be over. What ya done today will follow ya for the rest of your life. Nothing will grow where human blood has been spilled. That's what is gonna follow ya, Larraine. It'll follow ya back through the woodland and to the farm. Ya ain't made nothing better. The woodland and the farm are now spoilt by the blood ya shed."

We made the walk out of the woodland and to the farmhouse in silence. Once inside Cordie sat down in her rocker staring at the fireplace. I went to her closet and pulled out dry clothing for her but she didn't change. She sat in her wet clothing, said she had a chill and asked me to build a fire.

She was still there at the fireside when I went to bed. The rain and thunder left at midnight. I slept hard through the rest of the night and most of the next morning. That morning I found that the contents of all the closets in the house had been emptied and lay in piles on the floor. Cordie was in the larder moving jars of canned vegetables from one shelf to another. She was in the same clothes from the day before. Her muddy dress and blood stained apron now dry and wrinkled.

"Cordie, what are you looking for?"

"My sack!"

"What sack?"

"My cotton sack. I know it's here somewhere. It's almost noon and I should a been out picking cotton by daylight. Otha's gonna have a fit."

"Cordie, there is no cotton anymore. Remember, you and Otha stopped planting cotton years ago. I'll heat some water and make us breakfast. You need to eat, bathe and get out of those muddy clothes." She looked confused, then sad.

"Larraine, I don't know what I was thinking. I must be losing my mind. You're right, there is no cotton. No, Otha. No, Pity. All gone."

"You'll be okay, Cordie. You're tired. That's all. Some food and a bath will make you feel better."

She bathed, changed clothes but didn't eat. I gathered up her soiled clothing to burn, but she refused to let me.

"I may never wear 'em clothes again but they'll be a reminder of the day I got blood on my hands. Get some water and build a fire under my wash pot. I may be able to scrub the blood out of 'em clothes but never out of my hands, heart and mind."

Cordie spent two hours at the wash pot, rubbing her clothes up and down the washboard 'til her knuckles were bruised and bloody. With lye soap and all her effort the stains were still there when she hung the clothes on the line to dry. For the next week she rarely slept. Her mind wandered from past to present and sometimes the past and present were all together as if they both happened that very day. Temperatures were now in the eighties but she still asked for a fire. I could hear her at fireside praying long into the night.

TWENTY

The smell of Pity's body rotting in the well had dissipated, but I continued to bring water from the creek, boiling it for cooking and bathing. Cordie settled in to an existence of prayer, now day and night. Her hands became idle and I was lucky to get her to eat at least one meal a day.

One morning over breakfast she looked across the table then up at the ceiling.

"You want more coffee, Cordie?" She looked at me, lowered her eyes, picked up her cup, peered down into it, and then placed it back on the table, looking back at me.

"Larraine, do ya ever see his eyes?"

"See whose eyes?"

"James Lee's eyes."

"No, Cordie. I don't see his eyes."

"I do. I see James Lee's eyes. I see 'em most ever night. I wake up in the night and he's standing there at the foot of my bed, looking at me."

"Probably just a dream, Cordie. I buried James Lee. He can't come to the foot of your bed."

"Oh yes, he can and he does. He don't speak out loud to me but his eyes do. And ya know what his eyes keep asking me?"

"Cordie, don't talk like this. You need to put James Lee out of your mind. He's gone and we're safe now."

"I'll tell ya what his eyes say. They say, Miss Cordie, why did ya let Larraine do this to me? Ya knowed me since I was a kid. I ain't never done ya no harm. I want out a this hole. Find somebody to get me out a this hole?"

"Be quiet, Cordie! That's not James Lee! The devil is talking to you! Maybe you should read your Bible!"

I regretted the words as soon as I said them. At the same time I was terrified that she might tell Mr. Fields or a neighbor the same thing she'd just told me. Cordie sat, looking at me, her face almost childlike. Moments passed before she spoke again.

"Me and ya, Larraine, invited the devil in when we put James Lee in that hole. I been reading my Bible and praying but like I just told ya, James Lee comes most ever night now. He comes with his eyes asking me that same question. To find somebody to get him out a that hole." She left the table, went to the fireplace mantle, took down her Bible and began reading aloud.

Cordie spent her days reading the Bible and fasting. Some nights she would wake me, begging me to come to her room, saying James Lee was at the foot of her bed again. She lost half her body weight. She stayed indoors. The sun never touched her face. Her complexion paled and her beautiful silver hair yellowed. She had no interest in setting out new plants in our little garden or canning and filling the larder for the next winter. I grieved the lost days with her when she was my silver swan. The two of us on our knees, pulling weeds and setting out tender young plants along the rows. Her teaching, protecting and guiding me through life.

The last week of August I was surprised to see Mr. Fields truck coming down the lane. He had stopped coming by after Cordie refused his offers to take us on visits to Otha's grave.

I went out to meet Mr. Fields. He seemed nervous, standing with his hands in his pockets, looking down at the parched grass in the yard. There were moments of silence. The kind of silence where you knew the messenger was there with bad news. Silence that sent a chill up my spine.

I knew Cordie had not left the house, nor did she have a phone to reach out to anyone and tell them about James Lee. I also knew that by now James Lee had probably been reported missing. My mind raced through the possibilities of why Mr.

Fields had come. The worst of those possibilities was James Lee's body had been found so close to the farm. More moments of silence passed as the possibilities screamed inside my head 'til Mr. Fields cleared his throat and looked up at me.

"You and Miss Cordie doing okay?"

"Yes, sir. We're fine."

"Me and the neighbors been worried about Miss Cordie. She don't ever come to church anymore or ask me to take her to visit Otha's grave. None of us have seen her."

I felt a swell of relief. He'd just come to check on us, nothing more. I smiled and the lies left my tongue easily.

"Well, she has been a little under the weather from time to time, but I'm taking good care of her. Thank you for checking on us, Mr. Fields. I'd invite you in but Cordie's napping right now."

"Larraine, that ain't the only reason for coming today. I came to tell you and Miss Cordie that Ruby's in the hospital."

"Another one of her headaches?"

"No, Larraine, not this time. Your mama got the cancer on her brain. She ain't doing well. Doctors don't see her with much time left. I can drive you and Miss Cordie to the hospital anytime you want to go see Ruby. You let me know, okay?"

"I will. I'll tell Cordie as soon as she wakes from her nap and then let you know."

"I'm sorry to be the bearer of bad news. But you know Larraine, that your daddy, George is still on the drink and he ain't no comfort to nobody. He may not even know how bad off Ruby is right now. You and your mama may not have always been close but Ruby's dying and needs the comfort of you, her daughter and her mama, Miss Cordie."

"I understand. Thank you. I'll talk with Cordie."

Mr. Fields nodded his head, took a few steps toward his truck, then turned back to face me. "Oh, by the way, have you and Miss Cordie seen James Lee lately?"

That chill raced up my spine again. Lies back on my tongue.

"No."

"When was the last time you saw him?"

"Hmmm. I believe it was the summer before Otha passed. He stopped by to pick up some tomatoes for his mama from Cordie's garden."

"Well, ain't nobody seen him in a while. His mama and daddy are worried. But, 'tween me and you, everybody in the community knows James Lee better than his mama and daddy. James Lee is as hooked on the drink as your daddy, Larraine. James Lee's probably off somewhere drunk and ain't sobered up enough yet to show his face to his mama and daddy. He'll probably make his way home sooner or later. But, if he does stop by, you let me know and I'll pass it on to his folks that he's okay."

"I'll do that and thanks again for coming to tell us about Ruby."

So there it was. Word was out. James Lee was missing. I couldn't think about it and I sure couldn't tell Cordie that Mr. Fields had asked about James Lee. I knew the first words out of her mouth would be, "Yes, I've seen James Lee. He was at the foot of my bed last night."

But, I did have to tell Cordie about Ruby. I waited 'til the evening meal. I took a jar of canned corn and field peas from the larder, simmered them in a little butter and pepper, made cornbread and sweet iced tea and hoped Cordie would eat. She managed a couple of spoonfuls of peas and a bite of cornbread then sat staring at her plate.

"Cordie, Mr. Fields came by today."

"If he came wanting to take me to Otha's grave I ain't going. I told ya, I can't stand over Otha cause he'd know what's been going on around here. He'd know the awful things about poor old Pity in the well and what me and ya done to James Lee. I ain't going! So ya just walk down to Fields store and tell him that!"

"No, Cordie. That's not why he came. He came to tell us about Ruby. She's sick and in the hospital."

"Ruby? I don't remember a day in her life that she wasn't sick with one thing or another. Most of her ailments were only made up in her head. What's wrong with her this time?"

"Cordie, it's bad this time. She has brain cancer. Doctors don't think she has long to live. Mr. Fields offered to take us to see her."

"Brain cancer? A long time ago Ruby told me that one of her movie star friends had brain cancer and was gonna die. I guess she thought her mama was stupid. Ruby never had no movie star friends. I knew she got all that news out of 'em movie magazines she bought at the Piggly Wiggly. Larraine, do ya think that Ruby now believes she's got brain cancer just like that movie star cause she wants to be like a movie star?"

"No, Cordie. This is for real. Ruby has brain cancer and she's dying."

"Larraine, ya remember? She's had 'em headaches for years. She's always been a sack of nerves since she was born. I always thought it was her nerves and she needed to be put in a nervous hospital. That might have done her some good. I don't know. I've heard that nervous hospitals are awful places. Might have made Ruby better or might have made her worse."

"Do you want me to ask Mr. Fields to take us to the hospital tomorrow?"

"We'll wait a few days, Larraine. They'll give Ruby something at the hospital to stop her head hurting and she'll go home. We'll wait and maybe go see her when she gets home."

She rose from the table, unsteady on her feet. I got up quickly and grabbed her arms, afraid that she would fall. She pushed my hands away and stood staring into my eyes. Then she cradled my face in her hands and smiled. It was the first time that she had touched me or truly looked at me since the day I'd put the shotgun on my shoulder and kept it there and killed James Lee. Cordie's hands lingered on my cheeks, she leaned in closer and whispered.

"I love ya, Larraine. I've always loved ya."

My silver swan took flight that night. Her leaving was sudden but not really unexpected. It was as if something in the rushes had startled her, calling out, telling her it was true about Ruby and time for her to fly. It could have been the news about Ruby but deep in my heart I knew that I was just as much to blame for Cordie's leaving. I had taken her to a dark, unforgettable place in the killing of James Lee.

She had been grounded on earth and had lived two lifetimes. The lifetime before mine she had married and lost her husband to the Warrior River. She met my granddaddy, Otha, at that same river while washing out clothes in the shallows. In my life Cordie had been a matriarch, the keeper of children, a teacher and giver of comfort and love.

Now I find myself in her small country church with the smell of wildflowers and her neighbors telling me I should look upon her. They tell me it brings closure and helps with the grieving process. But I am not grieving and will not look upon her before the casket is closed nor see her take to the ground. My silver swan is already in flight and I know she will be back from time to time.

Maybe in the summer when the earth is green, the garden harvested and the sweet smell of honeysuckle fills the air, she will come. She'll be there on the porch among the rockers and porch swings with me shelling peas. Or in the cold days of winter she'll be there at the fireside in her rocker reading the Bible aloud.

In dreams she will come to me in times of despair and trouble, telling me all will be well. I know she will come and be with me and bring me comfort. I know because today before we left for the church she was standing at the edge of the woodland. Her arms were crossed, her hair silver again, her blue eyes shining and she was smiling and wearing the same blue flower print dress that they put on her for her taking to the ground.

I left the church and did not attend the graveside service. I walked home, back to the farm. Cordie wasn't in that wooden box that they were going to put in the ground. Cordie was home, on the farm and waiting for me. Mr. Fields and the neighbors arrived later. They brought food, hugged me and spoke of things that I no longer remember.

The next morning I found an envelope from Mr. Fields on the kitchen table among the leftover food. It was Cordie's will. She had left me the farm.

It took me two weeks to ask Mr. Fields to take me to Ruby's bedside. During those two weeks I could hear Cordie moving about the farmhouse, smell her biscuits cooking and see little signs, like the pages of her Bible open on the fireplace mantel. She was still on the farm and with me. Then the dream came. In the dream Cordie told me that a long season of death was ahead. And that she would be with me as long as she could.

Jan Fink

For a week I spent my days and nights at Ruby's bedside. At no time did Daddy visit. During that week Ruby grew weaker and more frail than one would think humanly possible. At one point I wanted to pick her up, free her of the hospital bed, the wires and tubes and carry her outside and hold her up to the sun.

I thought the warm rays of the sun would make her better, but Ruby was anchored by the war inside her head. I too was anchored. I could only watch and wait as her breath became slower and more labored.

On the last day of Ruby's war the walls of the private hospital room where they put the dying seemed much too bright. The room glared in its cleanliness like stadium lights, torturing my eyes and creating an unnatural heat. Ruby, her breath rattling from her chest went in and out of consciousness throughout the day.

She woke at eleven that night, staring up at me with wild, frightened eyes. When I took Ruby's hand to comfort her, I realized that Cordie was standing next to me.

Cordie whispered, "Tell Ruby. Tell Ruby, it's okay to let go and leave the pain behind. Tell Ruby, I'm waiting for her. Otha is here too. We're on the front porch at the farm. We're waiting. Tell Ruby, it's time to come home."

I leaned in close and gave Ruby the message. The room suddenly seemed cooler and not so white and bright. Ruby closed her eyes, her hand relaxed, the rattle left her chest and she grew still. Ruby's war was over.

Two funerals within one month. Ruby was buried next to Cordie and Otha. Daddy did not attend Cordie or Ruby's service. Mr. Fields told me that he'd heard that Daddy had been living in a flop house on the west side of town with a half dozen other alcoholics. Where Daddy was really didn't matter as long as he stayed away from me.

I spent days cleaning the farmhouse and moved my things into Cordie's room, hoping that she would come to me again. While going through her closet I came across an old flour sack, the top tied together by a long narrow scrap of quilting fabric. Inside there was change and cash amounting to five hundred dollars. It had to be every penny she was able to save from her days as a lunchroom worker.

Cordie had come. She was still taking care of me. But in that same thought, I wept because I knew her work was done. She had left me the farm and money enough to survive for a while, but she wasn't coming back.

I could grow my own vegetables, can them and stock the larder. Li'l Belle's milk was slowly drying up, but with the money Cordie left me I could buy milk and other needs from Fields Grocery. Members of the church had already come with field corn for the animals, firewood and kindling for the coming winter. I was content for now with this plan. The days passed slowly. I kept busy in the daylight hours but when night came and brought silence, I missed Cordie and Otha. I kept their rockers by the fireside hoping they would appear. The nights brought only the calls of the whippoorwills from the woodland.

A long year came and went and one late winter afternoon Mr. Fields came once more as the messenger.

"Larraine, your daddy, George, is in the hospital. The drink is taking his liver. He's dying. Do you want to go see him?"

I hadn't seen Daddy since Otha's burial. I wanted to ask Mr. Fields who was dying. Was it Daddy, the blue devils or both? But I kept silent and chose to go to Daddy's bedside.

We made the trip to the hospital in silence. Mr. Fields waited in the lobby. When I entered Daddy's room I thought I'd been given the wrong room number. The man in the bed didn't look anything like him. This couldn't be Daddy, tall and strong, who had pointed the rifle down at me that night and left me in the woodland when I refused to shoot the coon.

He was thin, his hair even thinner, his face as white as the hospital sheets. Blood slowly trickled from his nose and the corners of his mouth. The whites of his eyes were yellow. He looked up at me and began to cry. It was then that I knew that both Daddy and the blue devils were dying.

Out of nowhere a feeling of sympathy raced through me. He was helpless and I no longer feared him. I took a piece of tissue and tried to wipe away the blood, now mixed with his tears.

"Daddy, can you hear me?"

He opened his mouth to speak but when the words came it was not Daddy's voice. The blue devils spoke the last words.

"You'll never be rid of me. I'll be with you forever."

It took only a moment for me to know that I could no longer bear hearing the voice of the blue devils. I had no choice but to end their host.

I covered Daddy's mouth with one hand and with the other pinched his nose tightly. The blue devils had already taken him years before. Stripped him of mind, body and soul. There was no fight left in him. It took only minutes.

I went home no longer fearing Daddy or the blue devils. They were done. Daddy's brother took care of the funeral. Daddy was buried next to Ionia and Joe in their family cemetery plot miles from where Otha, Cordie and Ruby rested. I didn't attend the service. His brother had put Daddy in the very place he never wanted to be. I thought of the day when Grandfather Joe was buried. Daddy threatening us all with the promise that if we buried him beside his parents he would come up from hell and take us back down with him. I wondered if Daddy would do the same with his brother, the one who had placed him there next to Ionia and Joe.

Later, that week his brother brought me the clothes Daddy was wearing when he was admitted to the hospital. They were dirty, spotted with blood and smelled of whiskey. I built a bonfire that night and burned them. As I stood watching the last of the clothing burn a sudden wind rushed in. It picked up the ashes and smoke and carried them away. And I felt peace.

Within a year Li'l Belle's milk completely dried up. I added milk to the list of the few supplies I needed from Fields Grocery. I told Mr. Fields that Li'l Belle was no longer producing milk and he offered to buy her and have her slaughtered for meat. I said no, that I'd keep her as a pet.

He smiled. "Yeah, I guess it does get pretty lonely with Cordie and Otha both gone. Li'l Belle keeps you company and holds good memories for you."

Li'l Belle was good company and held many memories for me. Even when her milk dried up she'd call out each morning expecting me to be there milking her. I'd go down to the lean-to and spend time with her, rubbing her head and talking to her. One morning she didn't call out. I found her in the lean-to dead along with the rattler that had sunk its poison into her with four strikes. The rattler was coiled in the corner, its rattle singing. It took me five strikes with a dull hoe to kill it.

I left Li'l Belle in the lean-to and to nature. As Otha and I had left her mother, Ol' Belle, so many summers before after the tornado when we found her wrapped about an oak tree in the woodland. Nature takes care of these things.

TWENTY-TWO

After the rattler took Li'l Belle there was such a stillness about the farm. I missed her morning calls and as time passed I watched the pine supports of the lean-to rot away and drop and entomb her. The yard chickens disappeared one by one, taken in the night by coyotes and bobcats.

Other than the yard and my small garden plot I had no choice but to let the rest of the forty acres go untended. The grass, weeds and brush became head high in some places. It became a natural habitat for rattlers. I saw more of them every day. I filed down the best hoe I had 'til it was as sharp as a butcher knife and carried it with me at all times. The next summer I killed four rattlers within one week. On one of his visits Mr. Fields expressed concern about the rattlers and offered to bush hog for me. I turned down his offer. I had a plan for the rattlers.

Days later Mr. Fields was back with a puppy. "You wouldn't let me bush hog but at least give this pup a home. He's a just a mongrel but from the looks of him I think he's mostly feist. Feist are fast and good about letting you know snakes are around. In a year's time he'll be sounding the alarm if one of them rattlers gets anywhere near you."

I took the little mongrel and named him Mongrel. For the first six months he slept at my bedside on Pity's old quilt. He whined and whimpered most nights with puppy dog dreams. At a year old he was with me constantly, at my heels or running ahead, barking, sounding the alarm if so much as a field mouse or lizard was in the grass. He quickly learned the musk of rattlesnakes and knew they were near long before I did.

Mongrel didn't like anything or anyone other than me. He chased the chickens, Mr. Fields and the neighbors when they came near. I'd scold him and he'd back down but he stayed on guard, his ears up, at attention, watching for any sudden move in my direction. Early mornings he would leave my side and race through the pastures and into the woodland and bring back a squirrel or rabbit, dropping it at my feet. There was always meat to go along with the vegetables from my garden.

His obsessive love for me made us great hunters and natural born killers. And during the days of summer there were always rattlers to be hunted and killed. The farm offered them up, sometimes four or five in a day. In a way it was spooky, as if hell had opened a portal somewhere on those forty acres and the rattlers were using it. I didn't understand why but there had to be a reason.

The local high school started a bookmobile to reach and encourage more people in the community to read. It came to the farm once a month, stopping at the end of the lane. I was there, waiting every month, checking out books about rattlers. When I had finished all the books I knew the reason the farm was offering up the rattlers. There was money to be made from them.

I approached Mr. Fields. His store was the only one in the community and it had coolers and freezers and shelf space. He was reluctant at first but finally agreed to a consignment. I offered him a percentage of sales but he refused, saying that having such a novelty might bring more people to his store and they'd buy other items while shopping. He even put up a sign out front that read, "Now have genuine Alabama Rattlesnake Souvenirs and Rattlesnake Meat."

Mr. Fields gave me a large wheelbarrow so that I could bring my wares to his store. I started with the smaller kills, the young rattlers. I coiled them in Mason jars and preserved them with rubbing alcohol to be sold as souvenirs. The larger rattlers could be skinned, gutted, cut in sections, frozen and the meat sold. The skins could be sold for belts, boots or souvenirs. I kept the heads of the large kills and preserved them in Mason jars and kept them as trophies, nestled among the jars of canned vegetables in my larder.

It took a while for many people to embrace the rattlesnake meat but the rattlesnake Mason jar souvenirs flew off the shelves. Every summer it was a challenge for me and Mongrel to find the smaller rattlers. The large rattlers were always in abundance. I began preserving their heads in Mason jars and sometimes the entire snake in gallon jars and selling them for three times more than the quart Mason jars of smaller rattlers.

Mr. Fields and I ran ads in the nearest town's newspaper and people came out of curiosity, many going home with a souvenir. In four years I was able to have electricity run to the farm, indoor plumbing installed and a telephone.

Then one summer there were fewer rattlers. And the summer after that Mongrel and I encountered only two along the paths of our hunting ground. The second larger one taking me and Mongrel by surprise. It sunk its fangs into the calf of my right leg and slithered away quickly before I could make the kill. It took months to recover, sometimes in such pain I longed for death. My leg was never the same. I walked on an unsure leg like an aged woman.

TWENTY-THREE

Mongrel and I never went back to the hunt. The portal on the farm had closed, no longer offering up the rattlers. They simply disappeared. The earth on those forty acres had been saturated by their musk. You could smell it when the wind blew and taste it in your mouth on the hot sweltering days of summer. The earth in my garden refused to take the roots of new plants or seeds. The whole forty acres became a wasteland of dry parched earth.

In that last dream when Cordie came to me she had told me there was a long season of death ahead. The same summer that the rattler struck me, Mr. Fields passed away. He was buried in the same cemetery as Otha, Cordie and Ruby. His family called me to let me know they were closing Fields Grocery and asked that I pick up the remaining rattlesnake souvenirs.

For a few months I loaded the wheelbarrow and took it to the end of the lane at the farm. I sold a few souvenirs, but the effort of hauling them up and down the lane brought more pain to my leg than it was worth. What was left of the Mason jar rattlers I added to the shelves of my larder.

Idleness breeds loneliness. I wrote to Albert hoping for news about him, Sue and Miss Margie. The letter came back from St. Florian marked undeliverable. I looked up the number for the deli and a recording said it was no longer in service. I got the same recording for Miss Margie's boarding house. I felt guilty for not reaching out to them sooner. They had all moved on. To where or what fate I'd never know.

Mongrel and I were getting older. Idleness, loneliness, pain and age made time crawl. The days became longer and the nights brought fitfulness and nightmares. Unlike so many summers before on the hunt in the fields, now Mongrel and I spent the warm days on the porch. I brought the Mason jars of rattlers from the larder and placed them on the porch floor. We liked to look at them and sometimes Mongrel sniffed the lids and barked as if he were on the hunt.

On those summer days I looked out at the parched, dead fields and think of Cordie's words that day after I killed and buried James Lee. She told me that nothing would grow where human blood has been spilled. Maybe she knew what was coming and this time by my own making.

I thought of many things during those last summers. I thought of George and Ruby and how destructive and deadly their union had been. Little Brother, and the many nights we spent together in fear and hiding from Daddy and the blue devils. Ionia, who taught me how to fly to escape the bad times. Toxie, who opened her heart to me and opened my eyes to the sin of prejudice. Cordie and Otha, their life lessons and unconditional love. Johnny and the paint pony and our last ride into the woodland. James Lee, and his dark, cruel heart. I thought of them all, but only once. To think of them more than once only brought back mixed feelings. Love, loss, fear, hate and regret all rolled into one rush of memories that I chose not to repeat.

Had my heart long ago turned yellow and poisonous like the bitterweed? With the killing of James Lee had I destroyed the farm long before the rattlers came and left their musk? Had I become the very thing I dreaded the most? A natural born killer? Do I regret my actions and my survival?

I had spent fifty-three summers of my life on the farm. The farm was dying and so was I. The bite of the rattler had stayed with me and done its job well. Its poison was still in my veins slowly taking more tissue and energy day by day. I could do nothing more than remain on the farm with Mongrel and die along with the farm. And hope that Mongrel, like Pity with Otha, would be the angel that would take me to heaven. If there was a heaven I hoped it would be the front porch of the farmhouse, always summertime, sitting with Cordie and Otha. The fields lush and green, Otha telling stories and Cordie shelling peas.

For now, I can only tell you that in my mind I'll always be the child I never got to be. But I survived all who took my childhood away from me.

I was doomed from the beginning.

All my efforts were doomed by design.

My innocence was vulnerable to wickedness.

My innocence was my doom.